ENVY

By

Denise Hill

ENVY

DH Publishing Company
Indianapolis, IN 46220

ENVY
Copyright © 2017 by Denise Hill

Cover Design: Eric Strickland/Side Hustle Graphics
ISBN: 978-0-692-87348-9

Editor: DH Publishing Company
Email address:dhpublishingco@gmail.com
Website: www.dhpublishingco.com

ACKNOWLEGEMENT

Fourth Book!!!!

I want to thank God for another opportunity to write and publish another book. Writing is one of my passions and to know people are enjoying my work is very exciting. I appreciate all my readers and their feedback. I appreciate all the encouragement that I have received along the way, which is what makes me continue to do what I do and continue to do things outside the box. I want to thank my son and daughter for their continued support. I hope one day I can inspire others to step outside their box and do things they always dreamed about doing. You only live once so live for today and remember, never grow old with any regrets!

Prologue

Adriane couldn't take it anymore, she had to see Drake one more time. She had to know how he felt deep down inside of her. Adriane threw the covers off and removed her nightshirt. She grabbed a pair of sweatpants, a shirt and made her way downstairs. She quietly opened the front door and made her way onto the porch where she stood looking in the direction of the woods. The more she looked, the more she desired Drake and before she knew it, she was standing at his front door. Adriane paused before knocking, "What am I doing?" She asked herself loudly.

"I don't know, you tell me," Drake responded as he walked up behind her.

Adriane froze, she felt as if her heart had just stopped. She slowly turned around to face Drake, and when she did, she was greeted with a view of his hairy chest, washboard ABS and a kiss that made her lose her balance. No one had ever affected Adriane the way Drake had.

Drake swept Adriane up in his arms. He walked in the house and down the hall to his bedroom where he laid her on his bed. He stood above her and watched her as she melted under his stare.

Adriane watched Drake unfastened his belt and by the size of the bulge in his pants, she could tell he was packing. The size of his bulge was huge and for a minute she thought about getting up, but she knew if she did, she probably wouldn't get this opportunity again.

"What is it that you want with me, Adriane?"

Adriane removed herself from the bed to stand in front of him.

"I want you," she replied as she started planting kisses to his face.

"I want to feel you so deep down inside of me that you touch my soul. I want to take you in my mouth and watch as you come all over me. I want you to cry out my name as I fuck you like never before."

CHAPTER ONE

THE BEGINNING

Standing outside on the sidewalk in nothing more than her pajamas and her mother's diary in her hand. She stood frightened as the sound of sirens approached. She watched as the house that she once called home burned to the ground along with her parents. Adriane had no idea what life had in store for her, but she knew whatever it was, it would be better than the life she had here with her parents.

Adriane thought back to as far as she could remember and it wasn't a day that went by that she was not cursed out by her mom for one thing or another. She believed the first time she ever heard her mom call her a bitch was at the age of five. If it wasn't for her teacher calling her by her first name, she would have thought that stupid was her first name and bitch was her last name. What child at the age of five could do anything that was worth being called out of their name by anyone.

Adriane stood there with hate and anger in her heart for her parents. She couldn't understand why her mother did what she had done to her at birth.

Once the fire trucks and police arrived at the scene, some of the neighbors rushed out to see what was going on. One neighbor, in particular, had rushed to Adriane's side covering her with a warm blanket and a pair of their daughter's slippers. They had not been acquainted with their neighbor of eight years, but they were aware of who they were and with permission from one of the police officers, they took Adriane into their home to make her comfortable inside.

Adriane reeked of smoke after running inside the home to retrieve her mother's diary. This was the only evidence she had that would help her find her biological parents.

"Sweetheart, I am going to get you out of those nasty pajamas and into some clean ones if that's okay with you?" Mrs. Kane asked Adriane.

Adriane continued to sit in silence as Mrs. Kane ran her a bath and placed a clean pair of pajamas on the bathroom counter. Mrs. Kane eased the smoke-filled pajamas off Adriane and helped her into the tub where she began to bathe her.

Two hours later, there was a knock at the Kane's front door, it was one of the police officers.

The Kane's sat down with the officer where he questioned them about their neighbor, but unfortunately, they had no information to give him. The officer agreed with the Kane's that it would be in the best interest of Adriane if she stayed the night with them, but he assured them that someone from social services would be there in the morning for Adriane.

Late that night, Adriane lay awake in bed thinking about her parents. She wondered why someone would take a child from their birth parents at birth and raise them as their own to use and abuse them. Adriane was confused and she felt so alone right now. She had no idea what life had in store for her now and this frightened her.

Adriane continued to toss and turn as thoughts of her parents clouded her dreams. The sound of her mother crying out and the voice of her father calling out to her played repeatedly in her dreams. She could not get the look of terror on her mom's face and the way her dad tried so hard to get him and his wife out of the burning house.

Adriane stood on the bottom step after retrieving the diary from her room that she had taken a week ago from the attic in her mother's belongings and listened to the cries of her parents and did nothing to help them. She felt deep down in her heart that they deserved everything that was happening to them, she just wished she had done this sooner rather than later...

    The next morning social services transferred Adriane to a place she would come to know as home for the next ten years. The ride to her foster home was long, Adriane had no idea what to expect, everything had happened so fast that she had not had time to register in her mind the events that led to this day. She knew she had done a terrible thing, but she knew in her mind, this would be for the best.

She had suffered enough through the verbal abuse from her mother and the sexual abuse from her father, but the one thing that made her very angry was when she found her mother's diary and read that her mom had taken her from her biological parents at birth to raise as her own.

How could they take me from my biological parents and bring me into a household of abuse? The more Adriane thought about this the angrier she became which led up to her burning the house down along with her parents. Adriane had suffered for eight years, this was her only way to escape it all.

The car finally came to a stop, Adriane glanced up at the large brick house from inside the car, and her heart began to beat rapidly as she thought of a way to escape, but where would she go? The only relatives that she knew of were her biological mother, father, and her siblings and she had no idea who they were. She knew her mom's name was Deloris and that her mother, who raised her, was from Los Angeles and worked as a registered nurse before moving to Indiana. Adriane knew one day she would find her biological parents, she just hoped they would still be alive and had not forgotten about her.

Mrs. Johnson, who was assigned to Adriane's case as her social worker walked around to the passenger side of the car, opened the door and assured Adriane that it was okay to get out. After several minutes of persuasion, Adriane emerged from the car

and was greeted at the top of the stairs by Mrs. Oliver, her new
foster parent.

Mrs. Oliver looked to be about forty-five or so with dark
smooth skin and shoulder length hair. Mrs. Oliver was only a
few inches taller than Adriane. Adriane noticed her eyes more
than anything and the warmness she saw caused Adriane to be
more relaxed. Adriane knew she would be safe and loved here.

    Two months had passed and Adriane finally had adjusted to
her new foster parents and siblings.

    "Adriane sweetheart, you must finish your dinner before
you can go out and play, I don't know how many times I have
to keep reminding you of this." Mrs. Oliver said.

    "But I don't like peas." Adriane said as she walked back to
the dinner table."

    "Don't you know there are kids starving all over the world
and here you are wasting food?"

    "So why can't I send my peas to one of the starving kids"?
Mr. and Mrs. Oliver looked at each other and laughed.

    "Okay, I will let you slide this time young lady, but the next
time, I want your plate clean before you move away from this
dinner table"?

Adriane smiled as she got up from the table and ran outside to
join her foster brothers and sisters.

Adriane was the youngest of the six children and was not
allowed to go anywhere without one of the older kids, but
sometimes she would sneak away to visit a neighbor who lived
in the back of them.

Raymond was a young boy who was very mature for a 12-year
-old. He thought he was teaching Adriane things that a girl her
age shouldn't know anything about, but what he didn't know
was that she had already experienced these things with her
father.

Raymond had experimented sexually with Adriane. He had
done things to her that he had seen his parents do at night

when they thought he was asleep and on the other hand, Adriane had done things to him that her father taught her to do to him.

Adriane's behavior started to change and the Oliver's had noticed this right away. She became obsessed with her older brother. She would crawl into bed with him after everyone had gone to sleep, but he would march her little behind right back into her bed. It had gotten so bad that he had spoken to his parents about it after one night when he had awakened and found his penis in Adriane's mouth. From there on, the Oliver's watched Adriane closely, they had a little talk with her about it and found out that the neighbors' kid and her father had sexually molested & raped her and that she was just acting out what had been done to her on her older brother. The Oliver's explained to Adriane that this was wrong and that she must never let anyone touch her in that way, nor should she touch anyone else in that way.

"I thought it was okay Mrs. Oliver since my father touched me that way."

"Sweetheart, it is never alright for anyone to touch you, male or female, unless it's your husband."

Adrian looked confused. "Mrs. Oliver I don't have a husband."

Mrs. Oliver laughed. "I know, sweetheart, I mean when you get married."

It was the last day of summer and Adriane was excited about starting her new school. Her foster parents had taken her shopping and had bought her everything she had asked for, but the one thing she wanted more than anything in life was to be reunited with her biological parents.

Every night she would lay awake in bed wondering about her parents and her siblings. She wondered how they looked and if she looked more like her brother or sister. Her heart ached more and more each day until one day after she got home from school, she sat down and talked with her foster mom about it. Adriane entered the kitchen where she found her foster mom cooking dinner.

"How was school?" Mrs. Oliver asked Adriane.

"It was good."

"Then why the sad face?"

"Can I talk with you about something momma Oliver?"

"Sure, sweetheart, you can talk to me about anything." Mrs. Oliver said as she wiped her hands off with the dish towel and walked over to Adriane. Mrs. Oliver pulled Adriane to her and hugged her tight.

"What's troubling my sweet pea?"

Adriane opened her backpack and pulled out her mother's diary and handed it to Mrs. Oliver.

"I found this diary that my mom kept. She was not my real mother. She stole me at birth from my biological mother. I'm a triplet I want to know my biological family who lives somewhere here in Indiana."

Mrs. Oliver was shocked, to say the least. She couldn't believe what she was reading. "Oh, you poor baby. How could someone do this?"

By the time Mrs. Oliver finished reading she had tears in her eyes. Her heart ached for Adriane especially since these people abused her verbally and sexually.

Mrs. Oliver wiped the tears from her eyes, hugged, and kissed Adriane on her forehead.

"Sweetheart, go ahead and do whatever homework it is you have and when Popa Oliver gets home we will figure something out. I don't know how we will do it, but we will try and do whatever we can do to help you locate your family."

Adriane smiled and shook her head as she made her way to the family room to do her math homework.

She hated to think of leaving the Oliver's since they have been nothing but nice to her, but she had to find her biological parents even if it killed her.

Denise Hill

CHAPTER TWO

Weeks and weeks go by and no word from the Oliver's about the search for Adriane's family. Adriane was afraid to ask them about their search for fear of learning that they could not locate them or even worse, that they located them and they wanted nothing to do with her so she went on with life as best as she could.

TEN YEARS LATER

It was Friday afternoon and Adriane was in the best mood ever. She was glad it was Friday and was excited about attending one of her friend's birthday party the next day. Her foster mon had given her some money so she and a couple of her girlfriends could go to the mall after school to buy a birthday present and something for Adriane to wear to the party.   Adriane was busy talking with her friends on their way to the mall when Pete Johnson ran up behind her and hit her on her butt. Adriane turned around quickly and was about to slap whoever had hit her when she sees Pete. Pete was the most popular boy in school and was handsome as well. He had all the girls running after him.

"Boy, what is your problem hitting me on my ass like that?" Adriane said as she smiled from ear to ear.

"Aw, you know you liked it," Pete said as he hugged her around the waist as he walked with them.

"And where do you think you are going? I know your girl Katie would not approve of you walking with us, let alone you hugging me."

"I'm going where ever you are going and for your info, Katie and I broke up."

"Oh really, and when did this happen?" Adriane asked.

"About a week ago."

"Is that why you were at her locker earlier today?" Adriane's friend Renee asked.

"Damn y'all up in my business, but for your info, she was giving me my jacket back. Is that okay?"

"Right," Sharon said as she rolled her eyes at Pete.

"Can I take you to the movies tonight?" Pete whispered into Adriane's ear.

"I guess."

"Why don't you give me your number and I will call you right before I come."

Pete handed Adriane his phone so she can enter her number in it.

"Don't have me waiting all night," Adriane said.

Pete kissed her on the lips and said. "Now would I do you like that?"

Adriane watched as Pete ran back to his car. She has had a crush on him since fifth grade, but he never showed any interest in her. She wondered what Pete was up to because he had never said anything to her, but lately, she would catch him in class staring and winking at her.

Several hours later, Pete and Adriane walked into the movie theater to see Apollo Creed. To their surprise, the theater was almost empty, so Pete found a nice spot in the very back. Adriane snuggled close to Pete and laid her head against his chest. Pete was turned on by the smell of her perfume.

"What's the name of that perfume you have on?"

"It's a body sprayed called Velvet Sugar."

"Does your entire body smell this good?" Pete asked as he ran his hand across her perky breast.

"Yes, it does."

"Does it smell like that right here?" Pete asked as he ran his hand between her legs and under her thong.

"Oh, don't worry about them. My dad will be gone for the entire weekend and my mom passed away two years ago."

"Oh, I'm sorry to hear that. So did my parents."

"Really."

"Yeah, the Oliver's are my foster parents."

"Um… I didn't know that." Pete said as he escorted Adriane inside his bedroom and shut the door. He moved closer to her and started kissing her on her neck and moved down to her breast where he raised her crop top up and unfastened her bra. He took one of her breasts into his mouth as his hand made its way down to her thong and slowly pulled it down.

Adriane enjoyed the feel of him touching her body, she began to unfasten his belt and unzipped his pants pulling out his dick.

"What is a young man like yourself doing with such a big dick?"

"Sorry baby, but it runs in the family."

Pete backed Adriane up to the foot of his bed, turned her around and bent her over. He told her to get on her elbows and her knees,

he wanted that ass in the air as he ate her out from her ass to her pussy.

He had just finished eating her out when he slid his dick inside of her when his bedroom door opened.

"What the hell is going on in here?" Katie yelled as she flicked on the lights to see Adriane. "Oh, no you don't you fucking bitch."

She said as she ran towards Adriane, but Adriane was quick on her feet and pushed her away as hard as she could while Katie tried to swing at her. Katie landed on the ground, giving Adriane time to get her balance.

"I thought you said you and this tramp broke up?

"Adriane yelled at Pete as she fixed her clothes.

"Pete I want you to take me home right now."

"He isn't taking your trifling ass anywhere."

"He brought me here so he's taking me home."

"Pete, if you take her home, it will be over for us for good," Katie said in anger.

"But Katie, how will she get home, she can't walk home this time of night."

"I don't give a frog's fat ass how she gets home, but what I do know is that you will not be taking her. I want your ass out of here right now." Katie said as she moved closer to Adriane.

"Put your hands on me bitch and you will die," Adriane said.

"Then get the hell out of here."

Adriane looked over at Pete. Pete felts bad that he couldn't take her home, but he did not want to lose Katie for good.

"You're such a fucking loser and Katie, enjoy the taste of my ass on your boy's lips," Adriane said as she walked passed Pete and out of his room.

Adriane stood on the porch and phoned her older brother to come and pick her up. In the meantime, Adriane pulled out her box cutter, walked over to Katie's car and slit all four of her tires and proceeded to scratch her car from the front to the back of the driver's side.

The next day at the birthday party, Pete arrived alone. He knew Adriane would be here and he wanted to apologize to her for last night. He scanned the place until he laid eyes on here. She looked so pretty, he thought. He made his way over to where she and her friends were.

"Hey Adriane, can I speak with you in private."

"Fuck off dumpster juice." She said as she walked away. Pete laughed as he looked at her friends. I guess I deserved that."

"Yeah, you guessed right," Sharon said.

Pete turned back around to see where Adriane had gone and when he saw her, he walked over to her.

"I know I deserve whatever treatment you give me, but I just want to say I am sorry about last night. I shouldn't have gone out with you and I shouldn't have lied about not being in a relationship with Katie. I want you to know that I had the best time of my life with you last night and I hope and pray that one day, we can continue what we started."

Adriane looked at Pete, he could see the sadness and hurt in her eyes. She pretended to be tough, but he knew she was hurting.

"Can we be friends?" He said as he held out his hand.

"Friends like you I don't need," Adriane said.

"I see you are fucking with my man again," Katie said as she walked up.

Adriane looked at her and smiled. "I guess last night wasn't enough for you?" Adriane laughed as she walked away.

"You're going to pay for my tires and the scratch on my car," Katie said as she grabbed a hold of Adriane's arm. Adriane looked down at her arm and looked back up at Katie. The look that she showed Katie caused Katie to let her arm go. Adriane walked out front, pulled a cigarette from her purse and lit it. She was so furious with Pete and Katie that she needed a cigarette to calm her nerves. Adriane was out front for about thirty minutes before heading back to the party.

"Hey, there you are. We were looking everywhere for you." Sharon and Renee said.

"Are you okay?" Renee asked.

"I'm fine. I think I'm going to head home. I'm not really feeling this place right now."

"Do you want us to come with you?" Renee asked.

"No you guys stay and have fun. I will call you guys a little later."

Adriane walked home by herself. She took the short cut through the woods, which she was always told to never take this route, but right now, she wanted to get home as soon as possible. Adriane was almost home when she sees a guy on a motorbike staring directly at her. Now she wished she would have listened to her parents. Adriane slowly pulled out her box cutter from her purse and held it in her hand as she walked toward the exit of the woods when the guy called out to her.

"Hey, what are you doing trespassing on my property?"

"I didn't know this property belonged to anyone and I was just trying to get home quickly," Adriane said as the guy moved closer to her, blocking the exit. He looked her up and down. "Aren't you John's little sister?"

"Yes, I am."

"All right then, I will let you pass this time only?"

"Thank you," Adriane said as she took off running. Once Adriane was home, she ran upstairs to the bathroom and rinsed the brake fluid off her hands that had splashed on her. Adriane wiped her hands off and made her way to her bedroom that she shared with her older sister and laid across the bed and cried silently about Pete. She was so hurt by what had happened last night. She couldn't understand why God would continue to allow bad things to happen to her. She was angry and hurt.

Denise Hill

CHAPTER THREE

Adriane had drifted off to sleep and had awakened to the commotion that was going on downstairs.

Adriane rubbed her eyes and glanced up at the window to see the sun setting. She hopped out of bed and ran downstairs to find out what was going on. As she made her way into the kitchen, she saw Sharon and Renee talking to her family.

"What's going on?"

"We came over here to tell you Katie has been in a real bad car accident. I don't think she's going to make it."

"And you came over here to tell me this, why?"

"Adriane, where are your manners?" Mrs. Oliver asked.

"Mom, Katie was very mean to me last night. I had to have John pick me up because she wouldn't let Pete drive me back home. She wanted me to walk home by myself at midnight."

"Adriane, that's still no reason for you to be downright rude."

"I'm sorry mom, you're right."

Deep inside, Adriane wasn't sorry. She felt Katie got what she deserved.

Sharon and Renee follow Adriane out onto the front porch.

"So I ask you again and you came to tell me why?"

"We thought you would want to know."

"I could care less about the stupid bitch. Whatever happened to her, she deserved it for treating me the way she did."

Sharon and Renee look at each other.

"Adriane, you need to let that anger go and move on. We all knew Pete was lying when he said he and Katie broke up."

"No, I didn't know he was lying. I believed him. Do you guys think I would have gone out with him if I had known that?"

"No, I don't believe you would have," Renee said, but Sharon stood in silence. She had her doubts about Adriane ever since they met her as a little 8 -year- old.

"What about you Sharon?" Adriane asked.
Sharon threw both hands up in the air. "I'm sorry, but I thought you knew he was still with her and that you just didn't care."

"Oh, now I see what you think of me, Sharon."

"Whatever Adriane," Sharon said as she started to walk down the walkway.

Renee looked at Sharon and then back at Adriane. "You can leave Renee you don't have to stay behind with me."

Adriane always believed that it was Renee that was the glue that kept Sharon and Adriane friends for this long, but now she could see the glue slowly disappearing as their friendship slowly evaporated.

Adriane continued to linger on the porch looking in the direction of the woods. She wondered about the guy on the motorbike and why people were so afraid of him. She also wondered how he knew her and her brother. The more she thought about him, the more he intrigued her.

Adriane moved from the porch to the entrance of the woods. Adriane turned around to look back at the house before making her way into the woods.

Adriane was deep into the woods when she heard a noise behind her. At first, she was afraid to move, but when she heard the handsome voice speak, it eased the fear in her.

Adriane turned slowly as the man continued to question her about being on his property again, but when she turned to face him, she was greeted by a young man who was simply gorgeous she thought.

"I'll ask you again, what are you doing trespassing on my property?"

"I guess I wanted to know why people are so afraid to walk these woods."

"If you were smart you would be afraid too."

"And why is that?" Adriane asked as she moved closer to the young handsome man. "Are you the one that was on the bike earlier when I was passing through?"

"Yes and I told you I would let you pass just once, but I see you're back."

"Yeah, I don't usually take too well to threats," Adriane said as she moved to stand in front of the young man.

"Oh, did I threaten you?"

"Yes, you did."

"What do you want Adriane?"

"How do you know my name?"

The young man chuckled. "Who doesn't know your name. A pretty young lady like yourself who's well known on the east side of Indianapolis.

"Oh is that so."

"What I meant was since everyone knows your brothers, of course, they will know his siblings."

"So tell me something Mr."

"The name is Drake. Drake Stevens."

"Okay, Drake Stevens so why are people afraid to walk through the woods?"

"Years ago, my grandfather used to chase people in his wheelchair when he would catch them on his property. He hated when people would trespass on his property so ever since then, people have told many stories about the woods to keep their kids from trespassing."

"Oh, so he was a mean ass."

Drake chuckled again. "I see you have a way with words."

"You could say that."

"Well, my grandfather was a mean spirited person. People say his spirit lives on in these woods and that's another reason why people warned their kids not to cut through. But what I don't understand is why you decided to cut through and after you were warned, and then you come back."

"Well, like I said, I wanted to get home quick and I really don't like to be threatened, so I came back to see what was up with you."

"Curiosity killed the cat," Drake said, shaking his head.

"Well, I'm not a fucking cat am I?"

"You're something else I see."

"Yes, I am."

Drake started walking down the trail toward the house that stood at the top of the hill. Adriane followed slowly behind him not knowing what she was getting herself into.

Once they reached the top of the step, Adriane stalled. "What's wrong? You're not afraid are you Adriane?" Drake asked as he walked back to look at her.

"Of course not," Adriane said as the feeling of lust overwhelmed her. The smooth chocolate sight of his pretty face, the eyes of black coal and the smile that could warm anyone's heart played with her emotions.

Adriane took a step back. The nearness of him was too much for her to take.

"I think this was a bad idea. Why don't I let you be."

Drake led Adriane back to the entrance of the woods. "You're welcome to come by anytime Adriane."

"Thank you."

Adriane watched as Drake disappeared into the woods.

Later that night, Adriane laid in bed thinking about Drake. He was a real piece of work, she thought. She thought Pete was handsome, but Pete had nothing on Drake. Drake stood at 6'3 with a medium build. She couldn't get the sight of him out of her mind of how he looked in those jeans, bow legs and all. Adriane couldn't take it anymore, she had to see Drake one more time. She had to know how he felt deep down inside of her. Adriane threw the covers off and removed her nightshirt. She grabbed a pair of sweatpants, a shirt and made her way downstairs. She quietly opened the front door and made her way onto the porch where she stood looking in the direction of the woods. The more she looked, the more she desired Drake and before she knew it, she was standing at his front door. Adriane paused before knocking. "What am I doing?" She asked herself loudly.

"I don't know, you tell me," Drake said as he walked up behind her.

Adriane froze, she felt as if her heart had stopped. She slowly turned around to face Drake, and when she did, she was greeted with a view of his hairy chest, washboard ABS and a kiss that made her lose her balance. No one had ever affected Adriane the way Drake had.

Drake swept Adriane up in his arms, walked inside the house and walked down the hall to his bedroom where he laid her. He stood above her and watched her as she melted under his stare.

"What is it that you want with me, Adriane?"

Adriane removed herself from the bed to stand in front of him. "I want you. I want to feel you so deep down inside of me that you touch my soul. I want to take you in my mouth and watch as you come all over me. I want you to cry out my name as I fuck you like never before."

"You're a very bad girl I see," Drake said as he started to unfasten his belt.

"No Drake I'm a good girl. I'm good at everything I do." Adriane unbuttoned Drake's pants and released his 9 inches. She wrapped her hand around it and massaged the head with her hand before dropping to her knees.

Adriane took him in her mouth and worked her magic on him.

"Oh shit, Adriane! Aw, baby, you are good."

Before he came, Adriane removed him from her mouth and undressed. Adriane lay down on the bed and raised her legs, grabbed hold of her ankles and pulled her legs back leaving her pussy and ass in the air.

Drake moved toward her and slowly moved his hot wet tongue from the back of her ass to the front of her pussy.

"Oh shit, that feels so damn good. "Adriane yelled as Drake continued to please her orally.

"Drake please put that big dick inside me. I want to feel you deep inside me please!"
Drake pulled Adriane's body close to him as he guided his dick slowly inside.

"Oh my God! "Adriane yelled out.
Drake moved slowly in and out of her body as she took in all of his nine inches. He watched as he disappeared inside her tight, wet, juicy pussy and when he was just about to come, he pulled out and inserted his penis in her ass.

"No Drake no!" She yelled in pain as Drake continued to move in and out of her as his finger massaged her clit.
Drake began to move deeper and faster and all at once, he pulled out just in time to come at the crack of her ass.

"Baby, that was good."

The next day after school, Drake was parked outside the school as he waited to get a glimpse of Adriane. He waited for about ten minutes when he spotted her walking by herself. He turned on the ignition, pulled out of the parking space and slowly drove alongside Adriane until she noticed him.
Drake stopped his truck dead in his tracks when he sees her beautiful smile.

"You want a ride home?"

"Sure," Adriane said as she ran around his truck to the passenger's side.

"How was school?"

"Um... It was okay."

"You want to go and get something to eat?"

"I wish I could, but I have to go straight home. Can I come by your place a little later?"

"I guess that will be okay."

"What do you mean you guess?"

"I'm just playing with you. You are welcome anytime."

Adriane walked into the house, dropped her backpack in the den and made her way to the kitchen to grab a snack.

"Adriane whose truck were you getting out of?" Her eldest sister Marie asked.

"God, you are so nosey."

"No, you're just so secretive."

Mrs. Oliver waited to hear her response.

"Well, whose truck were you getting out of?"

"Mom!"

"It was Drake Stevens." One of her brothers blurted out.

"Now Adriane you know darn well that boy is too old for you."

"Mom age is just a number."

"I don't want you getting hurt by that boy."

"We're just friends and it was just a ride home. Jesus, you guys act like I just got caught having sex with him or something."

Adriane walked into the den where she flopped down beside her older brother John.

"You should not get involved with Drake you know that right?"

"Oh my God! Here you go. He offered me a ride home from school."

"So why did you seak out of the house last night to go see him? See, you have to be real slick to get anything pass me."

Adriane quickly turned to look at John.

"What are you talking about?"

"You know damn well what I'm talking about? Don't let me find out you're fucking him." John said as he placed his hand on Adriane's knee.

"You know I will be eighteen in two weeks right and then I will be free to see who I want, when I want and how I want," Adriane said as she winked at her brother and pushed his hand away.

Later that evening, Adriane snuck out of the house to go see Drake. She got a taste of him and now she craved him.
Drake stood in the doorway as he watched as Adriane made her way to him.

"for a minute, I thought you were going to stand me up." He said as he greeted her with a kiss.

"You have little faith in me, I see." She said as she kissed him on the lips. Adriane moved her hand down to the center of his body and grabbed a hold of his manhood. "Are you glad to see me?"

"Yes, I am," Drake said as guided her to his room.
Inside the room, the two could hardly keep their hands off of each other.

"Damn that was better than yesterday," Drake said as he lay on his back with Adriane snuggled up right next to him.

"You haven't experienced anything yet, just wait," Adriane said.

ENVY

CHAPTER FOUR

The next morning, Adriane awoke, she looked around the room and took in her surroundings when she realized she was still at Drake's.

"Oh my God! Drake where are you and why did you let me fall asleep," Adriane screamed as she ran from room to room looking for Drake. Adriane stopped when she heard the sound of a car door shutting. She stood frozen in place until Drake opened the door with breakfast.

"Drake how could you let me fall asleep."

"I'm sorry sweetheart, but when I realized you have fallen asleep, it was morning," Drake said as he made his way to her and kissed on the lips.

"I hope you don't get in too much trouble."

"I hope I don't either, but hell, what's done is done, I might as well enjoy myself because I don't know when the next time I will be able to come and see you."

"Babe, don't say that."

"I'm just being honest with you. I might be grounded until I turn 18 in two weeks."

"Oh, so you're not eighteen yet?"

"No, is that a problem?"

"Well, not for me, but your parents may have an issue with you dating a man twenty- five years old."

"Uh, probably so, but by the time they find out, I will be legal so there's nothing they can do about it."

"If you say so," Drake said as he walked into the kitchen. Adriane followed behind him and grabbed a hold of his butt cheeks.

"Oh, you're such a naughty girl."

"But you like this naughty girl."

"You damn right I do. Now sit down and eat your breakfast before it gets cold."

Just as the two begin to eat, Drake's front door opened and in came a pretty female that could pass for Adriane's twin.

"So what do we have here?" She said as she moved into the kitchen.

Drake turned at the sound of her voice. "Megan, what do you want? I thought I took that key from you," Drake said as he stood up.

Megan tossed the key on the table.

"Drake I need to talk to you."

Megan said as she moved to stand directly in front of Drake.

"Megan we have nothing to talk about and besides, I have company. You know what, you are so damn rude."

"Drake, I 'm not stupid. I can see you have company, but it won't take long."

Megan looked over at Adriane. "She' pretty. If I didn't know any better, I would say she's related to me."

"Well, it's good that you know better," Adriane said as she looked Megan up and down and rolled her eyes.

Drake laughed as he looked over at Adriane. "Adriane sweetheart, please excuse me for just a second while I get rid of our uninvited guest."

"Sure, whatever!"Adriane said as she sucked her teeth and continued to eat her breakfast.

Inside of Drake's bedroom, Megan grabbed Drake by the waist.

"I made a mistake."

"What are you talking about?" Drake asked as he took a step back.

"I made a mistake about us."

Drake laughed. "Well, guess what… it's too late to try and come back now."

"Drake you don't mean that. I know you still love me."

"I might still love you, but now, I know this right here, will not work. I've moved on like you asked me to. Now, as I said before, I have company so you need to leave."

Drake walked out of the bedroom and walked into the living to the front door. Megan stood in the hallway looking at Drake like she can't believe he's putting her out.

"Come on, let's go, Drake said, trying to be nice, but firm. Megan walked to the door. "Drake, think about what I said."

"No, you think about what you said," Drake said as he opened the door for Megan.

Megan walked, turned around and looked over at Adriane and smiled.

"Oh, it is nice to see my replacement."

"Honey, don't get it twisted. I am not replacing anyone. I'm too damn good to be a replacement."

Drake couldn't help but to laugh and then he looked at Megan. "Now do you need anything else? Goodbye, Megan."

Drake walked over to Adriane. "I told you, you have a way with words. I love it." He said laughing.

"Um… So how long have you guys been apart?"

"For about three or four months, but we were still sleeping with each other until two weeks ago."

"Why did you guys break up, if you don't mind me asking?"

"She wanted to run after her old boyfriend. She thought the grass would be greener on the other side, but I'm happy to say, she found out that it's not."

"Do you still love her?"

"No, I don't." He said as he moved closer to her and grabbed her hand.

"I found someone who I want to get to know much better."

"Oh really?"

"Yes, really," Drake said as he brushed his lips against Adriane's.

"You need to stop because if you keep this up, I may not ever leave."

"You don't have to."

"Yes I do and as a matter of fact, I need to leave now."

"Yeah, I agree because I don't want you getting into any trouble. Come on, let me walk you home."

Drake walked Adriane to the entrance of the woods and kissed her goodbye.

"Call me later," Drake yelled back to Adriane as she reached the sidewalk in front of her house.

Adriane stood in front of the door, debating whether or not she should go in, but just then, the door opened.

"Come on in here." Mrs. Oliver told her. "I see that young man got your nose wide open. I just hope you know what you're getting yourself into."

"Momma Oliver, I want you to meet him. You will love him. He's nice, considerate and he can be so funny at times."

"I just bet he can." Go on in there and get yourself some breakfast.

"I already ate. Drake brought breakfast for me."

Upstairs in the shower, Adriane thought back to last night. She loved her some Drake. She couldn't wait to see him later this evening.

Then she thought about momma Oliver, she was very much surprised at her behavior. She just knew she would get grounded, but as it turned out, Momma Oliver seemed to understand how Adriane felt about Drake.

Later that evening, Adriane stood and knocked at Drake's door. She knocked three times and no answer. She knew he was there because his truck was there and she could hear voices inside the house.

Adriane moved closer and was careful not to make any noise. She listened when she heard a female voice.

"Drake, how many times do I have to tell you that I'm sorry?"

Adriane stopped dead in her tracks. She could not believe who Drake was talking to.

"I told you time after time that we are done. I don't know how many times or how many ways to tell you or show you that I've moved on. Right now, I 'm seeing someone else."

"Who is she Drake? Are you and Megan back together?"

"No, Megan and I are not together and it's none of your business who I am with."

Adriane remained standing outside on the porch listening when something inside of Adriane brought out a rage that she always tried to keep from coming out. She banged on the door so hard that Drake and Sharon both jumped. Drake walked over to the door, opened it and was taken back when he sees Adriane. The one thing he didn't want Adriane to know was that he had been messing around with one of her friends. Sharon ran outside when she sees it's Adriane.

"Adriane, what are you doing over here?"

Adriane was so furious that she could not move or open her mouth to say anything."

"Adriane baby, let me explain," Drake said as he moved to hug her.

"Oh, I know you're not fucking this bitch," Sharon yelled out.

"Bitch, oh I got your bitch right here," Adriane said as she tried to move away from Drake.

"Stop Drake, let me go. This bitch has been asking for a good ass kicking for months and today is going to be her lucky day."

Drake continued to hold Adriane and he wouldn't let her go.

"How dare you bring your nasty ass over here. You're always trying to fuck somebody." Adriane said.

"Oh, no bitch you got a lot of nerves. Pete now Drake. Drake is my man so you better take your no good for nothing heartless ass home before I beat the black off of you." Sharon said.

Adriane lounged at Sharon and before Drake or Sharon knew it, she had punched Sharon in the eye and grabbed hold of her and put her in a headlock while she continued to beat Sharon in the head and face. Drake tried to break the two up, it took some time, but he was finally able to get Adriane away from Sharon.

"See, I told you to stop coming around here, but your hard headed ass wouldn't listen. I bet you'll listen now." Drake said as he guided Adriane inside the house.

"This isn't over Adriane."

"For your sake, it better be," Adriane said.

Inside, Adriane paced back and forth.

"How could you, how could you fuck a piece shit like her?"

"Adriane calm the fuck down. What's wrong with you?'

Adriane breaks down. She started crying uncontrollably.

"Jesus! That's what I get for messing with you young girls." Drake said as he moved to hug Adriane.

"Really Drake! I'm sorry, it's just... I need to go home."

That Evening, Adriane refused to come out of her room. Renee stopped by to talk with her, but she refused to see anyone. Mrs. Oliver tried her best to get Adriane to open up and talk to her, but again she wouldn't. Mrs. Oliver walked back down to the kitchen where John stood looking out the back door.

"John, can you try to get Adriane to open up to you? I hate seeing her like this."

"Mom, I'll see what I can do, but I can't make any promises."

John walked upstairs and knocked lightly on Adriane's door.

"Open up Dri. Do I need to beat Drake's ass? You know I will. Alright, I'm heading over to talk to Drake.

John stood outside the door quietly and waited. He knew she would open the door to try and stop him from going to Drake's.

Adriane unlocked the door, opened it slightly and stuck her head out and when she did John was standing right there.

"See you make me sick," Adriane said as she allowed John to enter.

"Now what's up with you. " John said as he walked in and took a seat on the bed. "You got mom worried. She said you came home running and crying."

"I don't want to talk about it."

"I told you not to get involved with Drake. Didn't I?"

"Right now, I am not in the mood to hear I told you so."

"Did he put his hands on you?"

"No, it's nothing like that."

"Then how did you get that scratch on the side on your face?" John said as he moved her face to the side to get a better look at her face.

"It didn't come from him."

"Then who? I'm not leaving until you tell me who."

"Man, me and Sharon got into a fight over at Drake's."

"What in the hell was she doing there?"

Adriane looked at John, shook her head and rolled her eyes. "I told you I don't want to talk about it."

"Either you talk to me or I will talk with Drake, your choice."

"Drake and Sharon used to mess around. She was over there trying to get him back or get fucked. So now, are you happy?"

John laughed. "Oh boy got all y'all acting crazy and shit."

"Whatever."

"Just be careful. I would hate for something bad to happen to you because of him, and then I would have to beat his ass. Get yourself together and come down and talk to mom. Let her know you're okay. Can you do that for me?"

"I guess."

Ten minutes, later Adriane walked to the kitchen to find momma Oliver sitting at the table with her head resting on the table.

"Momma Oliver, are you okay?" Adriane asked as she stood on the side of her.

"Yes, baby I'm just resting my eyes. Are you okay?"

"Yeah, I'm fine."

"It didn't look that way when you came running into the house earlier. Do you want to talk about it?"

"Not right now, but trust me, I'm good."

"Okay, but just know I'm here if you want to talk."

"Thank you, momma Oliver. I love you, I don't know what I would do without you." Adriane said as she gave momma Olive a hug.

Just then, there's a knock at the front door.

"I'll get it," John said who was in the den. John walked to the front door and sees who it is and walked into the kitchen. "Loverboy is at the door."

Adriane was shocked to find out that Drake was at her door. She was glad that her father was not home or he would have a cow.

Adriane took her time getting to the door. When she finally got there, she found Drake standing with his back to her with his hands in his pockets. She can't help but admire the way he looked from behind. He was sexy as hell, she thought to herself.

"What are you doing here?" She asked as she opened the screen door and walked out.

Drake walked over to her and put his hands up to her face. "I needed to see you, Adriane. I don't want things to end the way they did. Sharon shouldn't have been there. I apologize for that. Can you forgive me?"

"Why should I?"

"Because I'm truly sorry. I care for you and the one thing that I don't want to do is to hurt you."

"I can't believe you were messing around with Sharon's trifling ass."

Drake laughed. "I'm sorry, it's not funny. I fucked her twice and now she won't leave me alone." He said as he whispered into her ear.

"So why do you think it's funny? If I catch her over your house again, I will be so done with you and I mean it. Now laugh at that."

"You're too much," Drake said as he wrapped his arms around her waist and pulled her to him.

"You want to take a ride with me."

"Where to?"

"Don't worry about it. Do you want to go or not?"

"Sure, give me a minute to freshen up."

"Okay, take your time."

ENVY

CHAPTER FIVE

Thirty minutes later, Drake and Adriane cruised down 465 north. They were headed to Drake's sister. His sister was out of the country and had asked that he check on her place from time to time.

Adriane relaxed and enjoy the sound of Paul Taylor's Luxe live with Peter White. To be as young as she was, she loved her some jazz.

By the time they arrived, the sun had set and the warm breeze was blowing.

"Aw, this is so perfect," Adriane said as she looked over at Drake.

"It's perfect because we're perfect together."

"I could just sit here and listen to the music all night."

"We can do better than that," Drake said as he got out of the car and made his way around to the passenger side where he opened the door for Adriane.

"Follow me, your highness."

Drake led Adriane up the walkway to the front door. He unlocked the door and allowed her to enter.

"Oh my God! I love it."

"Yeah, I do too. Make yourself comfortable on the couch while I put some things together for us."

About ten minutes later, Drakes came back and swept her off the couch into his arms.

"This will be a night you won't forget, I promise." He said as he kissed her on the lips.

Drake took her outside on the deck where the hot tub was. He had candles lit all around the deck, he had food, wine, and smooth jazz playing.

"Oh, my," Adriane said as Drake started to remove her clothing piece by piece. He removed her shirt and then unfastened her bra. He planted little kisses to each breast before taking one into his mouth. He then moved down to

41

stomach planting kisses along the way. When he got to her belly button, he made love to it with his tongue.

"Oh Drake, what are you doing to me."

"I'm pleasing you that's what I'm doing."

Once Adriane was butt naked, she proceeded to do the same to Drake, but she started with kisses to his forehead. She moved down to his ears where she blew her warm breath inside before allowing her tongue to make love to his ear. This drove Drake insane.

" Damn, Dri."

Adriane laughed. He sounded so cute calling her by her nickname.

Adriane continued. She removed his shirt like he did, she took his nipple into her mouth until it became hard and then she proceeded to do the same with the other nipple. By the time she moved down south, he was long and hard as a pole.

"Looks like daddy is happy to see me."

"Yes, daddy wants so badly to get inside that tight pussy of yours."

"Well, I'm going to let you take your pants off, I wouldn't want to hurt that precious gem."

Drake laughed. "You are too much girl, I keep telling you."

Once Drake was free from his pants, he picked Adriane up and got into the hot tub with her.

"This feels like heaven. Have I died and gone to heaven?"

"Yes, you're in my heaven sweetheart."

Drake poured them a glass of white Moscato and made a toss.

"This is to a new beginning."

"Yes, to a new beginning," Adriane said as she took a sip of wine as she eyed Drake as if he was a piece of her favorite candy.

"Are you hungry?" Drake asked.

"Kind of."

Drake removed himself from the hot tub and pulled a cart close to the hot tub. He removed the towel that covered fried Chicken, potato salad, baked beans and dinner rolls.

"What! Where did you get this?"

"I already had this in my truck when I picked you up."

"Oh, so you just knew I was going to come with you."

"It was either you or Sharon."

Adriane gave Drake the evil eye.

"I see you're trying to kill this good mood I'm in."

"I'm just playing with you Dri. I want you in the best mood possible so when I put big daddy in you, you will take it with a smile."

Drake began to feed Adriane and she fed him. Adriane felt like this was a dream, it was just too good to be true.

"You know, I could spend the rest of my life with you if every day could be like this," Adriane said as she moved to stand in front of Drake.

"Drake, what are you doing to me? I have never felt like this before."

"I have to say, I feel the same way. I have been with plenty of women, but no one has made me feel the way you do. It's something special about you. Or maybe it's the way you work that ass on me."

"You are so silly," Adriane said as she splashed water on him.

Drake pulled her close to him. She sees the desire in his eyes and his voice is husky full of want.

"Baby, do you want me."

Drake looked at her without saying a word. He reached over to the cart and pulled out a can of whipped cream. He sprayed the whipped cream on her nipple and begins to lick it off devouring her nipple.

"Um... Drake that feels so good baby."

"I want to put this somewhere else."

"Go for it."

Drake picked her up and sat her on the edge of the hot tub and parted her legs, sprayed the whipped crème on her and ate her like this was his last meal.

"Drake baby, shit, oh Drake!" Adriane screamed out.

43

When Drake was finished, he looked up at Adriane. "I aim to please my dear."

"You sure in the hell do, but now it's my turn." Adriane took the whipped cream from him and told him to sit. She began to spray his penis with the whipped cream. She licked the tip and licked it clean. She took her tongue and began to lick each side of his penis until the whipped cream was nowhere in sight. Then she took him in her mouth and grabbed him by the base of his penis and took him in deeper and deeper.

"Damn baby do your thing."

Adriane had taken Drake to a place where he doesn't want to leave.

"Aw baby please don't stop. Take it all." Drake began pumping into Adriane's mouth. "Shit, this feels so damn good. Baby, I'm getting ready to come. Aw shit!"

Adriane stopped, removed her mouth and guided him to her vagina.

"Come on big daddy take good care of me."

"I'll do just that." But before he had a chance to get started his cell phone rang. He thought about not answering it, but it could be an emergency. He looked at Adriane.

"Go ahead and answer it. I'm not going anywhere."

"Thanks, bae."

"Megan, what's wrong? Calm down and tell me what's wrong."

Adriane looked over at him, rolled her eyes and got out of the hot tub. She walked over to where her clothes were and started to put them back on, but Drake tried to stop her.

"Stop!" She yelled.

"Okay, I will be there in about twenty minutes."

Adriane cannot believe what she just heard. This muthafucka is crazy if he thinks he's just going to keep playing me. I got something for that ass, just wait and see.

After Drake hung up with Megan. "I'm sorry bae. Something is terribly wrong and I need to see her and find out what's going on."

"Why the fuck do you care? Unless you're still in love with her. Are you Drake?"

"Don't ask me no stupid shit like that."

"Oh, so it's stupid. No, it's stupid that you're leaving me to be with a bitch that you don't fuck around with anymore. Or maybe you do. Maybe you're just lying to me. I'm done, you can take me home and you never have to worry about me anymore."

"Dri don't be like that."

"Don't fucking call me Dri. Only special people get to call me that and your ass ain't that special anymore."

The ride home was awkward, Drake felt like an ass for leaving to go to Megan's rescue, but he had a soft spot for females in trouble. He knew he had to find a way to make this up to Adriane. He just hoped she wasn't really done with him.
When he arrived in front of Adriane's home, he cut the engine and by the time he got around to the passenger side, she had hopped out and ran up to her front door, leaving him standing without saying good night, goodbye or kiss my ass.
Drake walked back around to the driver's side, opened the door and sat there a minute before starting the engine.
When he made it home, Megan was sitting on the porch waiting.
As he walked up, she stood and walked toward him.

"I'm so glad you came. I don't know what to do."
Drake stepped back and grabbed her hands. "What's wrong?"
Megan began to cry again. "I don't know what I'm going to do?"

"Megan, what's wrong?"

"I'm pregnant." She said as she looked at him with tear filled eyes.

The only thing that goes through his head was is it his.

"Megan, I need for you to be honest with me. Is this baby mine?"

"Drake, I don't know. I was sleeping with the both of you at the same time. I'm sorry Drake."

Drake felt like an idiot for leaving Adriane to be with Megan, who just confessed that she was cheating on him.

"Have you told your parents?"

"Of course not. How can I tell them? I supposed to go to college in the fall. I want them to be proud of me and now look what I have gotten myself into. I wanted to be the one to take their mind off of Michael, who is now serving a life sentence for murdering all those people. I have failed at doing that."

Drake paced back and forth. He was pissed and happy that he might be a father, but he really wanted to be with Adriane. "What can I do?" He asked himself.

"Have you thought about getting an abortion?"

"No silly, I can't do that."

"Why not?"

"Because I just can't."

"I'll pay for it."

"Oh, I see. Now that you're with someone new, you don't want anything to do with me or this baby."

"Megan, you and I both know that this could be Steve's baby. And I don't want to mess up a good thing that I have for someone who cheated on me and maybe carrying someone else's baby."

"Fuck you, Drake," Megan said as she turned to leave. "I will raise this baby by my damn self if I have to."

Drake stood on the porch and watched as Megan left. He was so confused about what to do about Megan's situation and his situation with Adriane.

The next morning, Adriane woke feeling sick. All she wanted to do was to stay in bed and cry, but she knew this was not an option. It was Sunday morning, time to get ready for church.

She knew Mr. and Mrs. Oliver were sticklers when it came to church.

"Adriane, hurry up so we won't be late." Mrs. Oliver yelled up to Adriane.

"I'm coming," Adriane said as she took her time coming down the stairs.

"Girl if you don't put some pep in your step." Mr. Oliver said.

"Good morning Dad."

"Good morning sweetheart." He said as he hugged her. "When we get back from church, you and I need to have a little talk. Just because I 'm not here all the time, doesn't mean I don't know what's going."

Adriane sat in church, in a daze. She could not believe what had happened last night. She thought Drake was a better person than that, but sometimes a wolf hides in sheep's clothing. She thought.

ENVY

CHAPTER SIX

When Drake woke he felt like a ton of bricks has landed on his head. He looked around the room until his eyes zeroed in on the time. The first person he thought about was Adriane, he wondered if she was up and if he called her, if she would answer. He called her anyway, but Adriane decided to leave her phone at home. She didn't expect any calls from anyone so there was no reason for a phone at this time.
Drake called three times and each time, his calls went directly to voicemail. Drake pleaded with Adriane to call him and to just hear him out. That's all he asked.

Later that afternoon, Adriane sat on the porch as she waited for Mrs. Oliver to finish cooking Sunday dinner.
Mr. Oliver made his way out onto the porch so that he and Adriane could have their talk. He pulled up a chair and sat right next to her.
"Just so you know, this is the same talk that I have with all my girls when they become a certain age. I love you dearly and I want the best for all of you, but I will not sit around and watch a man misuse any of my girls. If he caused you a lot of pain, then he is no good for you. You see how I treat your mother, this is how I want you to be treated by any man that you decide to lay down with. Now tell me about this boy Drake."
"There's nothing to tell. I won't be seeing him anymore."
"Why not."
"I don't want to."
"Did he put his hands on you?"
"No."
Adriane was about to cry, she did everything in her power not to let Mr. Oliver see how this affected her. She wanted to be strong so he would be proud of her.

John stood in the doorway and listened to his father and Adriane talk. He hated seeing her like this. John knew something was wrong between her and Drake, but this time, he was going directly to Drake.

John walked out the door and across the street. Adriane sat there and watched as he made his way through the woods to Drake's

house. She didn't even have enough strength in her body to move or say anything to him.

John knocked at Drake's door. He knocked twice before Drake answered.

"What's up John?" The way John was looking he could tell this was not a social call.

"Hey man, what the hell are you doing to my little sister? I tried to stay out of it, but I hate to see her hurting like this. If you can't do right by her, then I suggest you leave her the hell alone or else you and I are going to have some problems. And I guarantee you don't want any problems with me."

"Are you threatening me dude?"

"Naw, this is not a threat, it's a promise. I don't make threats I make promises that I do keep."

"You got a lot of nerve coming onto my property threatening me or making promises as you say, but I'm not the one you want to make threats or promises to, dawg. I think you have overstepped your boundaries." Drake said as he walked up to John.

"Don't walk up on me, man."

"Then you need to get the fuck off my property."

"Don't let me catch you calling or coming over to see my sister."

Drake stood there, he hated to get into it with John. But because of how he was feeling, things just went left. He normally doesn't let anyone get to him, but today was a different day.

Drake walked inside, he went straight to the refrigerator and grabbed a beer. He went back out on the porch and sat thinking about Adriane

Drake couldn't take it anymore, he got up and walked to the entrance of the woods and stood looking over at Adriane who sat on the porch with her father.

He wished he could relive yesterday, if he could, he would definitely do things differently. He would have put Adriane first and made Megan wait, baby or not.

Drake waited until Mr. Oliver went inside before pulling out his cell. Drake dialed Adriane's number. This time Adriane had her phone with her. Adriane looked at the number coming through and quickly deleted the call. Drake called again and again until he couldn't take it anymore and was in front of her house before he even knew it.

"Adriane, please talk to me, baby. Don't do me like this." Adriane continued to sit as if Drake didn't even exist. Adriane turned her head and looked the other way and before she knew it, Drake was on the porch standing in front of her.

"Damn, Drake," Adriane said as she turned around to find Drake standing right in front of her.

Adriane got up and tried to go into the house, but Drake grabbed a hold of her. Adriane please, just hear me out."

"Drake I don't give a rat's ass about you anymore." Drake had to laugh. "Don't be like that Adriane. I made a mistake. I'm human, I make mistakes from time to time. God can forgive me."

"Do I look like God?"

"No, but I know God lives inside of you. I know you're a good person that bad things continue to happen too. I just want to make you happy because you deserve it."

"Boy, take that bullshit back across the street with you and save that line for Megan or Sharon," Adriane said as she walked inside and shut the front door.

Drake stood on the porch looking at the door when it reopened. He thought it was Adriane, but instead, he sees

John. John was furious that Drake had the nerve to be on his porch after he warned him.

"I guess you didn't understand me when I said I better not catch you over here."

"John man, I am not trying to go there with you. I care for Adriane, I made a mistake. I came over here to apologize, that's all."

"Well, she doesn't want to see you or hear your apology so I suggest you leave while you can."

"You need to go somewhere with your threats. I'm telling you, John, you don't want none of this."

By this time, John was in Drake's face when Mr. Oliver walked out onto the porch.

"You two better stop all that nonsense." Mr. Oliver said as he walked up to the two. "Are you that boy Drake?"

"Yes, sir."

"John, go on inside, I want to speak with Drake alone."

John gave Drake the eye and said something under his breath before going inside."

"You know you got my family all in an uproar over Adriane. She's my baby you know and I will kill a man over her. Don't you dare miss treat or harm her in any way. Do I make myself clear, young man?"

"Yes, sir. I would never do anything to hurt her intentionally. I made a mistake in my judgment, that's all. I have not cheated on her, miss treated her or even put my hands on her. I would never do that, sir. I clearly made a mistake in my thinking."

"Is that so?"

Drake walked over and took a seat in the chair

"Last night, Adriane and I were at my sister's when my ex-called all frantic and I ended our night to go and see what was wrong with her. Now Adriane doesn't want to have anything to do with me."

"Is that the truth?"

"Yes, that's the truth. She's acting like I did something bad and now you guys think I did something to her."

Mr. Oliver took a seat next to Drake. "Listen here son, Any woman that's in your past, should stay in your past. If she was meant to be in your future or present she would be there. You have to determine if she's going to be in your present or future and if not, leave her in the past.

You know Adriane has had a bad childhood before she came to live with us. Life continues to throw bricks at her so we are very protective when it comes to her. It's time for her to get some enjoyment out of life. Sometimes, Adriane's heart is like an icebox, cold as all get out, but if you truly want to be in her life, you will have to melt that ice built up around her heart. It may take some time, but it can be done. And if you truly care you will do whatever it takes to melt it."

Mr. Oliver got up and touched Drake on his shoulder. "I have a feeling you know what to do."

The next morning Adriane walked to school by herself. Normally she would stop by Renee's and they would walk to school together, but today she did not want to be bothered with anyone.

Once she reached school, Adriane walked down the hall avoiding eye contact with everyone. She walked to her locker, got her math and science book out and when she closed her locker, Pete was standing there.

"Good morning, Sunshine," Pete said.

"Go fuck yourself."

"Damn! Why a brother got to go fuck himself?"

Adriane ignored Pete and walked into her first class which just happened to be the class he was in. Adriane took a seat in the first row and Pete took a seat right behind her just to irritate her.

"Damn you look good this morning," Pete said, poking Adriane in the back.

Adriane turned around and faced Pete. "Poke me again and I will break your fucking finger."
Pete laughed. "Sure you will. Hey, why don't you stop by tonight so we can finish what we started? I want a taste of that pussy again."
The boy sitting next to Pete started cracking up. "Damn, does it taste that good? Maybe I need to taste some."
"Maybe I need to put my foot up your ass," Adriane said as she turned to face her classmate.
"Damn, bae is ruthless."

Adriane's day didn't get any better because she had the two jerks in three of her other classes and to top that, her last class was with Sharon.
When three o'clock came, Adriane was out the school door quicker than you could say shit.
Adriane walked alone until Pete caught up with her.
Drake parked outside the school and watched Adriane and Pete walk home. He was furious to see this young boy with Adriane. Drake continued to watch until they were out of sight, then he pulled off and caught up to them.
"Hey Adriane, you want a ride?"
Adriane looked over at Drake and by the look, he had on his face, she could tell he wasn't too happy to see Pete with her.
"No, Pete's is walking me home."
Drake wanted to break Pete's little ass in half, but instead, he drove off.
"Now get the fuck away from me," Adriane said as she pushed Pete away.
"Damn, one minute you're hot and the next minute you're cold. What's up with you and that dude anyway?"
Adriane continued to walk and ignored Pete's question.
"Aw, so you're just going to ignore me."
"Yes, like I always do," Adriane said as she ran up the steps to the house.

Later that evening, Adriane sat on the porch looking in the direction of Drake's house. She wondered if he was home and if he was alone. She thought he would have tried to call her, but he didn't. She figured he was upset with her for walking with Pete.

Adriane continued to sit and look when she thought she saw something move in the woods across the street. So being the curious person that she was, she got up, made her way down the steps and walked across the street to the entrance of the woods.

She stood there looking to see if she saw anything, but when she didn't, she turned to leave and that's when she ran into Pete.

"Damn, what are you doing?" She asked Pete.

"I could ask you the same thing," Pete said

Pete backed her up into the woods. "Why are you playing hard to get Adriane, I know you want this dick."

"Boy boo. Stop acting like a yeast infection trying to get all up in me and be a good boy and go play because I don't play with little boys anymore. I have a man, a grown ass man. Now move out of my way, Pete."

"Not until you give me what I came for."

"Do you think I'm playing with you, boy."

"Boy, I got your boy right here." Pete pulled his dick out. Adriane started to back up and before she could run, Pete grabbed her and threw her down to the ground.

Adriane yelled, "Pete stop."

He straddled here, moved his hand up her skirt and ripped her panties. He parted her legs and was just about to enter her when he got a swift kick in his face.

"Get the fuck off of her."

Adriane looked up to see Drake standing there.

"Now if I ever catch you even looking at her, I will break your fucking neck. Do I make myself clear?"

55

Pete tried to stand.

"Do I make myself clear?" Drake asked again as he grabbed Pete by the collar.

"Yes," Pete said as he barely made his way out of the woods. Drake helped Adriane to stand. He grabbed her panties, swept her into his arms and walked toward his house. Drake carry's her in silence as Adriane rested her head against his chest. Once inside the home, he took her to his room and sat her down on his bed.

"Why did you bring me here?"

"You can go if you want to, I just thought we could talk."

"Talk, talk about what?"

"About us."

"Us, there is no us."

"Dri, I am sorry for everything. Like I said I made a bad decision. Can you or will you forgive me?"
Adriane sat in silence.

"Okay, I see. You can leave and you don't have to worry about me bothering you anymore."
Adriane eased up off the bed. She had too much pride to admit that she forgave him so she headed down the walkway to the entrance of the woods. She turned around to see that Drake had shut his front door. Her heart dropped to her stomach. She knew the right thing to do was to go back and accept Drakes apology, but instead, she turned back around and headed home.

Denise Hill

CHAPTER SEVEN

The following week, Adriane and her family made plans for her eighteenth birthday party. She invited a lot of friends from school and the neighborhood.

The day before her birthday, Adriane pulled the invite out of her bag that she had been carrying around all week. The invite was for Drake, but she was a little nervous to give it to him because of how things had ended between them. She was ready to take Drake back, just as soon as she delivered his invitation. Adriane got up enough nerves, walked across the street and through the woods to Drakes house. She took the steps slowly to his front door when she heard laughter coming from inside. She recognized his voice, but the female voice, she didn't recognize. Adriane was about to turn around and run when the front door opened. Drake stepped out onto the porch followed by Megan. Adriane opened her mouth but was unable to speak.

"Baby, you need to tell her," Megan said.

"Tell me what?" Adriane asked.

Drake hesitated. He didn't know how to tell her that when she left that day, last week, he had called Megan and they got back together for the baby's sake.

"Tell me what Drake?"

Drake still couldn't answer.

"Drake and I are back together and we're expecting," Megan said as she patted her stomach.

"Is this true Drake?"

Drake looked at Adriane, his heart was breaking. "Yes, it's true."

Adriane felt as if the world had stood still. Hearing the words coming from Drake's mouth was too much. Adriane turned to leave with her head hung low. The invite that she had for Drake slid out of her pocket.

Drake noticed it, but waited until Megan went inside, before picking the invite up. Drake pulled the invite out of the envelope. He felt like an ass right about now. His heart was with Adriane. He was only trying to do right by Megan after Adriane ended their relationship, now he regretted it.

Adriane walked into the house and the first person she ran into was John. By the look on her face, he could tell something was terribly wrong.

"Dri what is it?"

"Drake and Megan got back together."

"Come here," John said as he opened his arms. Adriane walked right into his arms. She was so hurt, but she can't even cry.

"Go ahead and cry, let it out. You will feel much better once you do so."

"I can't even cry, John. My heart feels numb."

"Well Lil sis, it looks like you just had your first heart-break. I wish I could tell you that this would be the first and the last, but I know that's not true."

"John, I will never allow myself to care for anyone as much as I cared for Drake, never."

"Never say never."

"Yeah, I can say never."

Later that evening, Adriane sat on the porch with Mr. and Mrs. Oliver. She sat there in a daze while the couple talked about things from their past. Adriane had always enjoyed hearing about them when there were younger, but right now, her mind was a million miles away. At times like this, she wished she knew her biological parents. She wondered if her parents were still alive and well. She knew if she was to ever find her parents, she would have to do some research of her own and she planned to do just that after her birthday.

The next day when Adriane woke up, she felt a little depressed. She wasn't really up for a birthday party, but so much time and money had been spent so she had no choice.

Adriane made her way downstairs and was surprised with a birthday breakfast. Everyone was sitting at the table waiting for her arrival.

"Happy Birthday," everyone said in unison.

"Aw, thank you guys, but you didn't have to do this. You already spent so much time and money on the party."

"This is a special time for you," Mr. Oliver said.

The tears that Adriane had been holding back came out uncontrollably. She felt horrible at such a special time in her life.

"Why did I let myself fall for him, why?" She questioned herself.

Mr. Oliver got up from the table and walked over and hugged Adriane.

"It's going to be okay Dri, everyone goes through what you're going through every now and then, just don't let it keep you down for too long. Here have a seat next to me.

That afternoon, Drake was at the mall trying to figure out something nice to buy for Adriane for her birthday. He still couldn't believe what he did. He wanted to slap himself over and over again. Adriane was so special to him and if anyone was to have his baby, he would have hoped it to be her, but instead it was someone who had cheated on him.

Drake walked into Victoria Secrets and went straight to the body sprays and lotion. He knew how much Adriane loved her smell goods. He purchased several different body fragrances along with the lotion and since he spent over 75.00 it came with a nice bag.

Drake then stopped by a hallmark card shop in the mall and purchased her a birthday card and a birthday balloon.

At four thirty, Adriane's backyard was packed with guest. They all waited for Adriane to come out so they could sing Happy Birthday to her.

"Girl if you don't get your slow behind outside." Adriane's two oldest sisters said as they walked into her room to find her sitting on her bed staring into space.

"Come on Adriane, you have got to get out of that mood and enjoy today. Worry about Drake's ass tomorrow," Marie said.

"Yeah, that's right. I see some pretty good looking young man out back," Trina said.

"I'm not thinking about any more men. I'm done," Adriane said as she got up from the bed and headed for the door.

"Yeah, that's what they all say," Trina said

"Just wait until you get outside," Marie said.

As Adriane made her way out back, she was shocked to see everyone in attendance. She looked over at the gift table and it is full of presents.

"Happy Birthday Adriane." Everyone screamed as they began to sing happy birthday to her.

Adriane's eyes watered, she was happy, but she was also sad. Adriane made a wish and blew out her candles. She wished she and Drake could be together, but now, she knows that is impossible.

Drake stood back in the woods, deciding on whether or not he should drop her gift off to her and leave it on the front porch or if he should give it to her personally.

Just then, Adriane walked around front staring into space. Drake made his way across the street and up the walkway in record time.

"Happy Birthday Dri," Drakes said, standing there looking sexier than ever.

Adriane looked up at the sound of his voice. Her heart melted.

"What are you doing here Drake?"

"I came to give you your birthday gift."

"Why Drake. Why did you do this to me?"

"I loved you, Drake. I would have done anything for you."

"I'm so sorry sweetheart. I thought I had lost you so I did what I needed to. I thought by getting back with Megan would help me get over you, but I was wrong. It just made me want you even more."

"You could have had me, Drake."

"Dri, I can't stand to be alone, so that's why I acted so quickly. I can make it right Dri. Just tell me you want me back. Tell me you still love me."

"You know I let my pride stand in the way the last time I was with you and I promised myself that I would never do that again. I promised myself that I would never love again either."

"Please, Dri, don't do this. I need you, baby, please." Adriane walked up to Drake. He can see the hurt and sadness in her eyes. Drake pulled her closer to him and began to kiss her. Adriane opened her mouth and allowed Drake to enter. Drake devoured her mouth as a moan escaped his mouth. "Oh Adriane baby, I want you so bad." And out of nowhere, Adriane pulled away.

"Is Megan pregnant with your baby?"

"She's pregnant, but I'm not sure it's mine. She was sleeping with me and another person. I guess she's hoping it's mine."

Adriane didn't know how she felt about the possibility of Megan possibly carrying his baby.

"So what happens if the baby is yours?"

"Just because she's carrying my child does not mean we have to be together."

Drake picked up her present and hands it to her.

"Happy Birthday Dri."

"Thank you, Drake." Adriane smiled with the biggest smile. I love you boo."

Adriane grabbed a hold of his hand and guided him around back with her other guests.

John stood there in disbelief with his girlfriend. "I can't believe this." John said to Pam."

"Oh get over it. You know how love makes you act sometimes. Let them be."
Adriane introduced Drake to Momma Oliver and her sisters. The two were inseparable the entire night.

Two hours later, the guest started to depart. Adriane and Drake were the only two left in the backyard. They brought in the last table and made sure all the trash had been picked up. Drake and Adriane make their way onto the front porch where they stand in each other arms.

"So did this day turn out the way you wanted it to?"

"Yes. I have to confess. When I made my wish before blowing out my candles, I wished that we could be together."

"Well, your wish came true."

"Did it?"

Drake looked down at Adriane. I can show you better than I can tell you."

"I'm going to hold you to that promise."

"Can you spend the night with me?" Drake asked in between kisses.

"What about Megan?"

"I'll handle Megan."

"Okay, because I don't want to have to kick a pregnant bitch's ass."

"You won't have to baby. I'm all yours. Just you wait and see."

Early the next morning around 3 am, Adriane woke to find Drake sound asleep as she lay in his arms. She looked up at him and smiled at the man who has stolen her heart. Adriane climbed on top and straddled him. She bent down to kiss him softly on the lips. She moved her way down to his chest where she licked each nipple until it hardens. She planted kisses along his midsection until she came to his penis. She began to massage it until it became long and hard. She licked the tip, the sides and then moved to his balls where she blew on them before she began licking each ball.

Drake started to stir in his sleep. He slowly opened his eyes to find Adriane staring back at him. He smiled before he pulled her down onto him.

"You're being naughty again, I see," Drake said as he flipped Adriane over and entered her quickly.

"Damn, I cannot get enough of this tight pussy."

"Drake, harder baby go deeper. Aw shit baby, that's it."Adriane screamed out.

"Let me get on top," Adriane said.

Adriane got on top and she started twerking on Drake ass.

"Damn girl do your thang."

Adriane rose up slowly off of his dick and came down on Drake quick.

"Aw shit, that feels so damn good."

Adriane continued to ride Drake until he came hard.

"Damn that was one good nut. If I didn't know any better, I would say you're trying to pussy whipped me."

They both laughed.

The two lay in bed talking and listening to Paul Taylor's Dry your eyes.

"Man, Paul Taylor is a bad dude."

"Yes, he is. You have to see him in concert." Drake said.

Drake rose up. "I have something to ask you, but you don't have to give me an answer right away. I just want you to think about it, Okay. Once you graduate, will you move in with me?"

"What if I said I was going away to college?"

"That's cool. You can move in once you graduate from College."

"Then I would say yes."

"You sure do know how to make a man happy," Drake said as he leaned over to kiss Adriane.

Denise Hill

CHAPTER EIGHT

Weeks later, Katie passed away. She was on a ventilator for three weeks and when she was taken off, she passed away two days later. Pete was so upset and blamed himself for her accident. She was mad at him about the night she caught him with Adriane and decided to drive to the party herself. Normally he would have driven her. The police ruled this as an accident her brakes went out and she was not able to stop her car from colliding with a semi. It looked as though she had no brake fluid…

A week after Katie's funeral, Pete returned to school just in time for graduation. He took Katie's death hard and it also made him think about his mom more. He hated funerals and made a promise after attending Katie's funeral, that he would not attend another funeral unless it was his dad's.

"Welcome back Pete." Mrs. Sampson said as Pete walked into class.

"Thanks."

Adriane sat there in class and watched as Pete walked in. She didn't fill any hatred for him and for some reason, she felt guilty for what she did to Kate's car. Since being with Drake, she has softened up a lot. She was beginning to enjoy life.

"I am sorry to hear about Katie," Adriane said as Pete took his seat in the back of her.

Pete was taken back with Adriane. She had never said anything nice or even been concerned about Katie since the accident.

"Thanks."

Adriane felt good being able to let go of the anger that she harbored for Pete and Katie. I guess being with Drake had really removed the ice from her heart.

Later that evening, Adriane was at home in her room getting ready for graduation when Mrs. Oliver walked in.

"I just wanted you to know how proud of you I am." She said as she handed Adriane a small box.

"Momma Oliver you didn't have too. You've done so much for me since I have been here."

"I can't believe you are all grown up, getting ready to go to college and leave the nest."

"Momma Oliver, there's something I need to tell you. I decided to stay here and Indianapolis and go to school and move in with Drake."

Momma Oliver was shocked. "Is this really what you want to do, Adriane?"

"Yes, I love Drake and I don't want to be a million miles away from him. But I will make you one promise and that is to graduate from college. I will not let anyone or anything stand in my way."

"Well, as long as you keep that promise, I can live with you moving in with him, but you know your dad. He may be a different story."

"Oh, I can handle old softy," Adriane said as she kissed Mrs. Oliver on the cheek. "I don't know what I would have done without you."

Adriane opened the box that Momma Oliver had given her. It was a necklace with a pink diamond in the middle.

"I love it, Momma Oliver. You know how much I love the color pink."

"Yes, I know. When I saw it, I knew I had to buy it for you."

"Thank you so much!"

The graduation ceremony was held at the Bankers Life Fieldhouse and it was packed. Renee and Adriane were so excited about this day. They stood by each as they waited patiently for their turn to enter the stadium.

"Okay, people, let's get lined up."
Adriane stood in front of Renee as they marched into the
stadium. There were so many people that Adriane had no idea
where her family and Drake were seated, but she knew they
were there and that's all that matters. She couldn't believe that
after today, her life would be forever changed in more ways
than one.

That evening at Drake's, the two celebrated, but the
celebration was short- lived when Megan lets herself in.
"Oh, so this is why you've ignored my calls."
"Megan, what are you doing here? I told you it was over."
"Like hell, it is," Megan yelled as she walked over to Drake.
Do you think just because you're with this little bitch that
you're just going to say to hell with me and this baby? Do you
Drake?"
"Wait just one minute," Adriane said as she moved closer to
Megan.
Drake stepped in between the two women.
"I got this baby, let me handle this."
Adriane folds her arms and stood while Drake handled the
situation with Megan.
"I'm going to make this loud and clear just this one time. I
don't want anything to do with this baby until you can prove to
me that its mines. Do I make myself clear? And another thing,
you will not come over here anymore unless I invite you and
you know that will not happen."
"Oh, and we need that spare key back since I will be living
here now," Adriane said just to rub it in.
Megan laughed as she threw the key at Adriane.
"You're such a sorry bitch," Adriane said as she picked the
key up off the floor.
"Yeah, and you're even sorrier. Enjoy my leftovers."
"Oh, don't worry, I will. I will do more than just enjoy. I will
fuck his brains out every chance I get."

Drake shook his head. He was cracking up on the inside. Adriane had a way with words that would tear you inside and out. She knew what buttons to push and she knew when to push them.

"I see you're a smart mouth bitch. If I wasn't pregnant, I would show you a thing or two."

"Honey, just pretend that you not pregnant. I'm all for learning a new thing or two even from the dumbest people."

"Who you calling dumb. I will fuck your little ass up."

"Really, you and what army?" Adriane asked as she moved to stand in front of Megan. "Go ahead and give me your best shot so I can fuck your pregnant ass up."

"Oh, you would just love for me to lose this baby, wouldn't you? You know this baby will always be a part of Drake's life and you cannot stand that can you?"

Adriane came this close to telling her little secret that would throw a monkey wrench in Megan's plan, but she decided to keep it a secret just a little longer.

"Puff, be gone bitch," Adriane said as she threw her hand up. "You know what Megan, you're starting to act just like a little homeless puppy. You feed the little mutha fucker and now you can't get rid of it."

This time Drake couldn't contain his laughter. He laughed so hard that Megan got so furious and stormed out.

"Woman, you are something else," Drake said as he walked over to Adriane, pulled her to him and kissed her lips. "But that's why I love you so much."

"Well, since you love me so much. Will you help me locate my biological parents?

"I don't know what I can do, but whatever you want me to do, I will do it just for you."

"You're so sweet."

"Yeah, me so horny too!"

"Oh my God, you're so crazy."

"Crazy about you," Drake said as he wrapped his arms around Adriane and guided her into their bedroom.

Drake undressed Adriane until she was completely naked. He kneeled down in front of her and pulled her closer and then he looked up at her.

"Do you know what would really make me happy?"

"No, what would really make you happy Drake?"

"If you were to have my babies."

"Oh, really."

Drake stood up and looked at Adriane. "Yes, that would really make my life complete and if you would accept my hand in marriage," Drake said as he pulled out a tiffany box and opened it. It was an 18K Rose Gold diamond ring.

"Oh my God! Drake this is gorgeous. I love it!"

"Well, will you marry me, Adriane Lynn Pruett?"

Adriane was so focused on the ring that she never heard Drake's marriage proposal.

Drake grabbed Adriane by the shoulders.

"Sweetheart, did you hear what I just asked you?"

"I'm sorry, what did you say."

Drake laughed. "I just asked you to marry me."

Adriane laughed.

"I'm sorry, right now I'm so overwhelmed, but I would love to be Mrs. Drake Stevens."

Adriane said as she kissed Drake.

"Damn, I'm a happy man right now," Drake said as he picked Adriane 2 feet up off the ground and swung her around.

Adriane loved how the rose color gold band shined in the light. "This ring is so gorgeous."

"It's just like you? I got this the day I got your birthday present."

"What! How did you know I would take you back?"

Drake rubbed his hand across his face. "I knew how much you like the D."

Adriane burst out laughing. "You are too much."

Adriane walked over to her purse and pulled out a pink and white box.

"I wanted to wait until later to tell you this, but since I'm going to be Mrs. Stevens, I feel it's only right that you know right now."

Adriane hands Drake the box.

"What is this?" Drake asked.

"Open it and found out."

Drake opened the box and began reading the instructions.

"Are you serious?" Drake asked as he looked up at Adriane.

Adriane nods.

"Damn, I'm the man," Drake said as he walked around the room with the biggest smile on his face, but then, he turned around and looked over at Adriane. "Do you know without a doubt, that this baby is mine?"

"Drake, I'm not Megan. I have not slept with anyone while I was sleeping with you."

"You know I had to ask."

"I understand."

"How long have you known?"

"I found out the day I came over here to invite you to my birthday party, but when I found out that you and Megan had gotten back together, I decided to get an abortion."

"What!"

"What was I supposed to do? Raise this baby by myself and put all my dreams on hold so I could be a single mom. No, that was not happening."

"You would not have had to raise the baby by yourself. I would have been there for you."

"I didn't know that. All I saw was you and Megan and the baby she's carrying."

Drake scratched the back of his head. "Man, I am so glad you didn't abort my baby. Do you know what I would have done if you had and I found out?"

"What would you have done?"

"There's not need to go into that since you didn't abort daddy's baby."

"Naw, I want to know what you would have done to me," Adriane said as she walked to stand directly in front of Drake.

"I wouldn't have harmed you in any way if that's what you think. I don't believe in putting my hands on a woman to harm her."

"I just wanted to make sure."

"Is there anything else I need to know?" Drake asked Adriane.

"No, but I need a favor and I want to talk to you about some things."

Drake guided Adriane back to the bed so they could sit and talked.

"What is it that you need?"

"I need to find a job for the summer before I go back to school. I need a car and like I asked you, I would like for you to help me find my biological parents."

"Why do you have to work?"

"Because, I want to pull my own weight around here until I start school in the fall."

"Baby, I am the man of the house. I got you. And you don't have to worry about a car. I have a nice car in the garage that I have been working on, it's yours if you want it and yes I would love to help you locate your parents. How do you think the Oliver's will feel about you searching for your parents?"

"I don't think they would mind."

"Is there anything else?"

"No."

"Good, cause I need to put this D up in you."

Adriane laughed loudly

"That's my baby daddy."

Denise Hill

CHAPTER NINE

It was Adriane's last week living with the Oliver's so she and Drake decided that this was a good time as any to break the news to them about the engagement and the baby, but before they did Drake wanted to ask her dad for his hand in their marriage.

Mr. Oliver and Drake sat out on the porch talking when Drake asked the question. Mr. Oliver looked out into the open area, he looked up and down the street before looking at Drake.

"I know you can provide for her and I know you love her, but why are you two getting married so soon?"

"Well, as you know… I'm just going to come out and say it. Adriane's pregnant and I want to do the right thing by her and my child."

Mr. Oliver got up from his seat, walked over to the door and opened it. He made his way inside where he found Mrs. Oliver, Marie and Adriane in the kitchen talking. Mr. Oliver stood there looking at Adriane.

"I knew there was something different about you girl." Mr. Oliver said as he walked over to Adriane and put his arm around her shoulder.

"Hot damn, I am going to be a papa." Mr. Oliver shouted! Once Drake heard the laughter, he entered the kitchen to join in.

"Congratulations Drake," Marie said.

Momma Oliver walked over to Drake and hugged him as she whispered in his ear. "Please take care of my babies."

"Adriane held up her ring."

"Oh my God. You're getting married too." Marie asked.

"Of course, silly. Did you think I was going to be a single mom?"

"Drake asked me for my blessing and I'm giving it to him now, Congratulations son." Mr. Oliver said as he patted Drake on the back.

Just then John walked in looking at Drake sideways. "What are we celebrating?"

Adriane walked over to John. "You're going to be an uncle." And then she held up her ring. "I'm going to be Mrs. Drake Stevens. I just love the sound of that."

John stood there unable to speak. "Um... Well congrats baby sis," John said as he hugged Adriane and walked out of the kitchen.

"John, what's wrong with you?" Adriane asked as she followed behind him.

"Nothing. I'm happy for you."

"But you didn't say anything to Drake."

"Was I supposed to?"

"Yes, he's going to be your brother in law."

"Lucky me."

"John," Adriane said as she shook her head.

"I hope he's not marrying you just because you are pregnant."

"He's not. He asked me to marry him before he knew I was pregnant."

"Well, I'm happy for the both of you and my little niece or nephew."

"Thank you, John. That means so much to me. Come on back in the kitchen and celebrate with us." Adriane grabbed a hold of his arm and guided him to the kitchen. By this time, the entire clan was there celebrating.

Adriane took the last box of her belongings to the truck. She made her way back up to the house to say her good bye's to the family.

Mr. & Mrs. Oliver had tears in their eyes.

"Come on now. It's not like I'm moving out of state. I'll be just right around the corner. You will see me every day, I promise." She said as she turned to leave fighting back her own tears.

The next morning, Adriane felt weird. Everything had happened so quickly that she hadn't had time to soak anything in. First the graduation, then engagement, the pregnancy and today she and Drake will begin their search for her biological parents.

When Adriane looked around, Drake was nowhere to be found. Adriane got out of bed, stood and then stretched and before she had a chance to do anything else, she got a pain in her stomach. She rushed to the bathroom where she vomited.

"Oh my God. Please don't let this happen too often."

"I see my baby girl is having morning sickness," Drake said as he walked in with breakfast in hand.

"Hey babe, whatcha got?"

"I got you some pancakes, sausages, eggs and orange juice."

"That sounds so good. I'm so hungry I could eat a cow."

"Why don't you get yourself together while I set the table."

"Okay."

Adriane ran a warm washcloth over her face and attempted to brush her teeth. She gagged the entire time.

Adriane headed to the kitchen when something red outside caught her attention. She walked over to the front door, opened it and to her surprise, there sat a red 2014 Kia Sorento parked out front.

Adriane walked into the kitchen.

"Whose SUV is that parked out front."

Drake pulled a pair of keys out of his pants pocket and handed them to her.

"That's the car I was telling you about."

"Are you serious." She asked as she took the keys from him.

Drake smiled. "I told you I was working on it."

"Yeah, well, I thought it was an older car, not an SUV that looks brand new."

"It's not new. It's a 2014 model."

"Thanks, babe," Adriane said as she walked over and hugged and kissed him on the lips.

"I hope you brushed your teeth."

"Ha ha," Adriane said as he punched Drake in the arm.

"I'm just saying while you're trying to kiss a brother and all."

Adriane sat down to eat. "Are you still going to help me with the search for my parents?"

"Yes, ma'am. I think we should start with the local library and look through their archives."

"Sounds good. I'm so excited."

"Just don't get your hopes up, babe. I don't want to see you get hurt."

"The only way that can happen is if I find them and they want nothing to do with me."

Later that afternoon, Drake and Adriane arrived at the Indianapolis Public Library. They enter the parking garage.

"Dang, this is kind of confusing down here."

"I know. Okay, there goes a parking spot right here."

Drake and Adriane took the elevator up to the main floor.

"OMG, it's so big in here. I have no idea where to begin." Adriane said as she stepped off the elevator and looked around.

Drake walked over to the information desk.

"Excuse me, can you help us?"

"Sure, what can I do for you?"

"Do you guys keep copies of death certificates in your system?

"No, but I could order one for you. What's the name of the death certificate?"

"Um… I'm not for sure?" Adriane said. "I know the mother's first name is Deloris."

"Deloris," Drake said under his breath. He knows that Megan's mom's name is Deloris and that she lost one of her triplets at birth.

Drake wiped his hand across his face. He hoped his suspicions were not right because if it was, he was going to have a big problem on his hand that could cause him to lose Adriane if he found out Megan is her sister. Hell, they look so much alike, he thought.

"Do you know the date of the death?"

"I have a date, but who's to say it's correct."

"I guess we have hit a road block," Drake said.

"If you can try and find out the name on the death certificate that would really help me out."

"Okay, thank you so much," Adriane said.

Adriane and Drake walk away. "You know Drake, I don't even know if I was reported dead or stolen. So we need to check old news articles for that year to see if any newborns were stolen at birth just in case."

"I thought you knew for sure that you were reported dead?"

"No, in my mom's diary, she said she had taken me. I just assumed she reported me dead to my real parents."

"Oh well, this changes everything. Let me do some checking on my own this week and I will let you know what I find out."

"Thanks, Drake, I really appreciate your help."

"Babe, I would do anything for you and I hope you believe that."

Adriane looked up at Drake and smiled. "What did I do to deserve someone like you?"

Drake chuckled.

"What's funny?" Adriane asked with her hands on her hips.

"You are," Drake said as he pulled her to him, bent down and kissed her on the lips. "I love you so much Dri. I've never felt this way about anyone. I don't know what it is you're doing to me, but whatever it is, don't stop, please don't."

"I love you too Drake. I never thought I could love someone this way, but you changed me. You changed me on the inside."

"Naw, the D changed you on the inside." He said as he laughed.

Adriane looked at Drake.

"Seriously Drake. I'm trying to be serious and all you can do is joke."

"I'm sorry babe, but you opened yourself wide open for that one."

"Yeah, I guess I did," Adriane said as she laughed and grabbed a hold of Drake's hand.

"Let's bounce." She said

Drake and Adriane waited patiently for the elevator and when the doors opened, Megan stepped out.

"Look who we have here." She said as she moved to stand in front of Drake.

"Hello, Megan," Drake said.

"Hello Drake, how are you?" Megan said as she looked over at Adriane.

"I'm good and you?"

"I'm doing well for someone pregnant."

Adriane laughed as she held up her hand displaying her ring to Megan.

Megan looked back at Drake.

"Really Drake. We were together for how long and I never got a ring. How could you do this to me, Drake, when you know how I feel about you? I'm carrying your child Drake."

"Well, right now, we don't know if that's Drake's baby or not," Adriane said as she pulled Drake inside the elevator as they both stood and looked at Megan as the elevator doors shut.

ENVY

CHAPTER TEN

A few days later, Drake pulled up to Megan's house. He sat for a minute before getting out. He was not sure he really wanted the answers to the questions he was about to ask Megan and her parents. What if what he suspected was true and what if it tore his relationship with Adriane apart. He wouldn't be able to live without her in his life.

Drake got out of the car, looked around before he slowly walked up to the front door. Once he was there, he rang the doorbell twice before Deloris opened the door.

"Well hello, Drake. I'm surprised to see you here."

"Hey, Mrs. Brown how are you?"

"I'm doing good for an old lady. How have you been?"

"I've been doing good. Is Megan here?"

"No, Megan is not here."

"Okay, can I have a minute with you?" Drake asked.

"Sure, come on in."

Drake followed Mrs. Brown into the family room.

"Have a seat," Mrs. Brown said. "So, what can I do for you, Drake?"

"I have some things to ask you, but I am not trying to dig into your past or open any wounds, but it is very important that I get the answers to these questions if you don't mind."

"I will try to answer whatever I can."

"Megan told me stories about her being a triplet. Is that correct?"

Mrs. Brown looked at Drake. He could see the sadness in her eyes.

"I hate to bring this up, but it's very important."

"Why is this important Drake? Why is bringing something up from my family's past, so important to you?"

"I can't say right now, but once I am finished researching I promise, I will tell you."

Mrs. Brown sighed. "I don't know Drake."

"Mrs. Brown, just trust me. I know it might be hard talking about this."

"Okay, Drake, what is it that you need to know?"

"Was your baby stolen at birth or were you told your baby died?"

Mrs. Brown thought back to 18 years ago. "Well, the nurse that helped deliver my babies was a black female in her late thirties. I will never forget her. She was the one that told me my baby had

died, but for some reason, I didn't believe her. I tried several times to reach the doctor that delivered my babies, but I was unsuccessful in reaching him because that was actually his last day working here in the United States."

"Did you have to sign a death certificate or was there one? Had you already given her a name before you found out she had died?"

"No, we didn't have to sign anything and yes, we had already named our babies."

"What was her name and what happened to the body?"

"That same nurse told me that they had burned my baby's body in the incinerator."

Drake looked at Mrs. Brown.

"I'm sorry, we were young and we didn't know any better back then."

"What did you name her?"

Mrs. Brown allowed the tears to fall. "I'm sorry Drake, this is still so painful for me."

"I know and I'm sorry, just take your time."

"I will never forget her. She was so special. She had two deep dimples and her eyes were so dark that they looked gray. The last time I held her, she held onto my finger so tight. I guess she could sense that this would be her last time in my arms. I would give anything to go back in time so I could hold her just one more time."

This touched Drake to his core.

"Okay, Mrs. Brown," Drake said as he stood and wiped his eyes.

"That will be all. I'll be in touch." Drake said as began to walk to the front door.

"Drake, I never told you her name. Her name was Reagan."

"Thanks, Mrs. Brown," Drake said as he made his way to his car.

The next couple of days, Drake thought about what Mrs. Brown had told him about her baby. He had a feeling that Adriane was her daughter. Should I say something to her or should I keep it a secret? Drake wondered.

Just then, Adriane walked through the door.

"So how did it go?" Drake asked as he walked over to kiss Adriane on the lips

"It went well. I think I got the job, I just have to wait for them to make me an offer." Adriane said as she put the bag of groceries and her purse down, and removed her shoes.

"That's good, but you know you don't have to work."

"Drake, I want to pull my weight around here. Just because I 'm pregnant, doesn't mean I can't work or go to school."

"I know. I'm just saying."

"So how did your day go?" Adriane asked as she started unloading the groceries.

"It was an interesting day, to say the least."

"Did something bad happen. Let me guess, you ran into Megan?"

"No, it was nothing like that. I'll talk to you about it after dinner.'

"Okay."

Drake walked into the kitchen. "Why don't I help you with dinner," Drake said as he walked up behind Adriane and grabbed her by the waist.

"Shit, you can help me with more than dinner," Adriane said as she turned to face Drake. "I want some of this." She said as she grabbed his crotch.

"You can have that anytime you want. Just tell me where you want it."

Adriane unfastened Drake's belt and unbuttoned his pants. She pulled out his member and got down on her knees. I want this right here." She said as she took him in her mouth.

"Aw shit. Girl, you show know how to please your man. Damn!"

Before he came, Drake removed himself from Adriane's mouth. He picked her up and placed her on top of the table and pulled her close to him as he entered her.

"Baby I want all of it." She said as Drake slowly entered her.

Drake moved slowly in and out, deeper and deeper. "Aw shit, give it all to me. Drake, I love you so much." Adriane said between breaths.

Minutes later, Drake collapse on top of Adriane.

"Damn, ain't nothing liking having dessert first," Adriane said.

"You're going to get more dessert after dinner. I just wanted to give you a taste." Drake said as he kissed Adriane on the forehead.

After dinner and another session of lovemaking, Drake and Adriane lay in bed cuddled up with each other.

"This is so perfect," Adriane said as she looked up at Drake.

"I know."

"I can't believe I had never seen you before I walked through the woods that day."

Drake laughed.

"I saw you the first day you arrived at the Oliver's."

"What!"

"Yeah, I knew all about you. I watched you grow into a beautiful woman."

"So why didn't you ever say anything to me?"

"Oh, believe me, I was going to approach you sooner or later. I used to ask Sharon about you all the time, but she really wouldn't tell me anything about you. I guess she wanted me for herself.'

"That bitch."

"Adriane, that's not nice. You're a better person than that. Don't hold grudges, please."

Adriane looked up at him. "I guess you're right because I'm the one that got the prize."

"Yes you did and so did I. Good things come to those who wait and I waited a long time for you," Drake said as he ran his finger down the middle of Adriane's face.

"Now can I have some more dessert?" He said as he moved between her legs.

The next morning, Adriane woke feeling sick to her stomach. "Oh God, not again." She said as she rushed to the bathroom. After vomiting, Adriane sat down on the floor with her back up against the bathtub with a wet washcloth to her mouth wondering when will the morning sickness end. She had a doctor's appointment next week and she would be sure to ask the doctor about how long does the morning sickness last because she was already over it.

Adriane was just about to get up off the floor when she heard the doorbell ring.

Adriane walked quickly to the front door to find Megan standing outside on the porch.

Adriane opened the door and looked at Megan with a smirk on her face.

"What do you want Megan? My fiancé is not home, he's at work."

Megan laughed.

"Is there something funny Megan?"

"You think you've won don' you?"

"Won, won what? Is this a game or something?"

"You may have Drake now, but when this baby is born, let's see who has who?"

Adriane laughed because Megan has no knowledge of her pregnancy.

"Whatever Megan. Is this what you came over here to tell me?"

"No, I came over here to talk to Drake and ask him why he came to see my mom yesterday questioning her about my dead sister."

"What?"

"I don't appreciate him upsetting my mom like that because that happened 18 years ago, that's the past and that's where we want to keep it, in the past."

"Well, since I know nothing about that, I can't say why he's concerned, but I will pass your message on and if he wants to call and talk to you about it, he can," Adriane said before shutting the door in Megan's face.

"You stupid bitch!" Megan yelled.

Adriane stood on the other side of the door laughing at Megan."

"Go find another home you homeless little puppy dog," Adriane said as she opened the door back up.

Later that evening Drake arrived home. "Hey, babe," Drake said as he leaned over to kiss Adriane who's sitting in the recliner watching TV.

"What took you so long to get home and what's in the bag?"

"I worked a few extra hours over and don't worry about what's in my bag," Drake said jokingly.

"Guess who stopped by today?"

"Who?"

"Megan."

Drake had a strange look on his face.

"She wanted to know why you came over yesterday questioning her mom about her dead sister."

"Um... Is that all she said?"

"Pretty much, oh, she did tell me that once her baby was born, we would see who gets you. I just laughed and slammed the door in her face, which really pissed her off."

"I can believe that. Did you cook anything?"

"No, not yet."

"Don't worry about it, I'm taking my favorite girl out for dinner."

"Good, because I don't feel good at all. I've been sick all day."

"Aw, my little baby is making my big baby sick."

"Yes, she or he is. I will be so glad when I get past this phase."

ENVY

CHAPTER ELEVEN

At dinner, Drake was contemplating on telling Adriane what he had in the paper bag, but he didn't know how to tell her without getting her hopes up, so he decided to find another way to get her to take the DNA test without her knowledge. He had no idea how to get Mrs. Brown to do this without telling her what he suspected. The last thing he wanted was for Mrs. Brown to tell Megan, and Megan run and confronted Adriane about it.

"How's your dinner, babe?"

"It's delicious. How's yours?"

"It's good. I think I'll be coming here more often." Adriane laughed. "You took the words right out of my mouth. I can't believe I've passed this place a million times and never thought about stopping in."

"A couple of my employees told me about this place last year, but I forgot all about it, until this afternoon."

"What happened this afternoon that made you remember?"

"I saw it when I was at lunch today and I decided to bring you here for dinner."

"I'm so glad you did."

"Oh, before I forget, I have a doctor's appointment next week, do you want to come with me?"

"I would love to. What day and what time?"

"It's next Wednesday at 1."

That night while Adriane was asleep, Drake took the box out of the paper bag and removed the swab. He walked over to the bed where Adriane lay asleep. He nudged her a little just to make sure she was asleep and when she didn't move, he took the swab and ran it on the inside of her cheek for about 60 seconds.

He took the second swab out and did the same thing, before placing both swabs back inside the container. He then placed the container back inside the paper bag and took it outside, to his car and placed it in his glove compartment.

The next day at work, he phoned Mrs. Brown and Megan answered the phone.

"Hello Megan, can I speak with your mom?"

Drake why are you calling my mom and why are you trying to bring up the past? Leave it alone, Drake." Megan yelled before hanging up.

Drake waited ten minutes and then he dialed the number again, hoping Mrs., Brown answered and to his surprise, Mrs. Brown answered.

Drake told her about his suspicions and asked that she keep this between the two of them until he knew for sure. He also asked her to meet him Saturday, so she can take the test as well.

Mrs. Brown was on pins and needles. She was so eager to find out who Drake believed was her daughter. She can hardly keep this news to herself, but she promised him not to tell anyone until they knew for sure.

When Drake arrived home, he pulled up to find Megan sitting on the hood of her car waiting for him.

As he got out of the car, Megan walked toward him and by her expression, he can tell she is upset.

"What the hell are you trying to do Drake?" Megan asked.

"Megan, what are you talking about?"

"You know damn well what I'm talking about. Why are you contacting my mom? Leave her the fuck alone. Don't let me have to tell you again."

"And if I don't what are you going to do?"

"Don't make me hurt your precious Adriane, Drake."

"Girl, don't come over here making threats."

"Don't make me do something I will regret."

"Naw, don't make me do something to you that I will later regret if you ever try and harm Adriane."

"You really love her don't you, Drake?"

"Yes, I do."

"Why couldn't you love me like that Drake?"

"I did. Actually, I loved you more, but you didn't know how to accept my love. You always wanted more, you thought the grass was greener on the other side, and now look at you, you alone and pregnant."

"I know better now Drake. I now know how to accept your love."

"It's too late Megan. I will never leave Adriane for anyone," Drake said as he walked toward the house.

"Drake please, give me another chance." Megan cried.

"Megan, I am engaged to be married to Adriane and we are expecting a baby."

"What! That fucking whore! How dare you do this to me, Drake. How can you have a baby with anyone besides me? How could you?"

"Megan, go home."

"You bitch ass nigga," Megan said as she charged at Drake and hit him in the back and jumped on him and continued to throw punches at him.

Adriane was in the house cooking when she heard the commotion. She walked to the front door and sees Megan on Drake's back beating him. Adriane ran out the door, she forgot all about being pregnant as she ran to Drake and grabbed hold of Megan by the hair and pulled her off of Drake and onto the ground.

"Bitch, what the fuck are you doing to my man? You must be fucking crazy coming over here trying to provoke him into beating your ass. He won't hit you bitch, but I will." She said as she stomped on Megan's face.

Drake pulled Adriane away from Megan and carried her inside.

"Calm down baby, calm down," Drake said as he hugged Adriane.

"Baby you can't be fighting and shit. I don't want to lose my baby over some bullshit."

"You better keep that bitch from coming over here if you know what's good for you and her."

Drake threw his hands up in the air. "Damn, here you go with the threats."

"No, I don't make threats. I make promises." Drake laughed, he remembered John said the exact same thing. Adriane walked into the kitchen and turned off the stove. She was so furious that she refused to finish dinner. "You can get your own dinner now." She said as she walked down the hall to the den.

"Why am I in the dog house?" He said as he followed her down the hall.

"Because you can't keep your bitch from running over here every time I turn around, that's why."

"Dri, I can't control what Megan does."

Adriane looked at Drake crazy.

"So you're saying she can just waltz her little ass over here anytime she wants and there's nothing you can do about it. Is that what you're saying because I know I can do something about it?"

"No, that's not what I'm saying."

"Then explain it to me, because that's what I'm hearing."

"I'll handle it."

"You better or I promise I will."

"My little fighter, but I don't need you fighting my battles for me, especially since you're pregnant."

"Come here." Drake said as he stood in the entry way of the den."

Adriane looked at Drake debating on whether to ignore him or go to him. She looked at him and noticed how sexy he was looking, so she made her way to him.

"What?"

"Don't be mad at me. I didn't do anything wrong. I was just a little upset with you trying to fight in your condition. That's all.'

"And I 'm tired of Megan coming around here. I have had five encounters with her and that is too much. I feel like I should just ask her to move in here with us."

"Oh, I see you're a comedian now."

"I'm not trying to be funny. How would you feel if Pete continued to come around here, sniffing up my ass?"

"Oh, I already handled him so I'm not worried about him coming around her."

"But you get pissed when I try to handle Megan."

"Naw, babe, it's not like that. If you were not pregnant, then I wouldn't say shit. I'd let you handle your business, but you're carrying my baby and my baby momma should not be fighting anyone in her condition."

"Ugh, I hate being called baby momma, just call me Adriane."

"Okay, I can understand that. I'll just call you Mrs. Stevens. Is that better?"

"Hell yeah."

Drake smiled.

"So now can I have some sugar?"

"You can have whatever you want."

Saturday afternoon, Drake sat in Star Bucks waiting for Mrs. Brown. He only hoped she hadn't changed her mind. He continued
to sit as he sipped on his Iced Vanilla Latte when he spotted Mrs. Brown's car pull up.
Drake looked around just to make sure Megan's crazy ass wasn't somewhere hiding. Mrs. Brown walked through the door, she looked around for Drake.

"Mrs. Brown," Drake said as he waved her over.

"Hello, Drake," Mrs. Brown said.

"Hey, Mrs. Brown. I wasn't for sure if you were going to show up or not."

"I gave you my word that I would be here and I didn't say a word to anyone about our meeting, but Drake, I need to know who the young lady is that you think is my daughter. And how do you know my child didn't die at birth?"

"Well Mrs. Brown, I can't be sure she is your daughter and that your daughter didn't die, but what I do know is that the young lady that I am referring too, found out, that her mother that raised her for eight years, stole her at birth and that she was a triplet. She found all of this information in her mother's diary before she died. She knows that her birth mom's name is Deloris. So I kind of put two and two together."

"Oh, I see. So how will we know for sure?"

"I purchased a DNA kit and I have already swabbed her mouth, now I need to do yours and have it sent to a lab to determine if the DNA's match."

"How long will it take for the results to come back?"

"We can have the results back as fast as 1-2 days."

"That's good. So what do I need to do?"

Drake pulled out the paper bag with the DNA kit in it. He removed two swabs from the container.

"I'll need to swab the inside of your cheeks."

"Is that all?"

"Yes, it's as simple as that."

Drake took the swab and ran it alongside the inside of her cheek. Then he took the second swab and did the same thing. Once he was finished, he placed the swab back into the container.

"That will do it."

"Will you call me as soon as you have the results?"

"Yes, I will."

"I can't believe this is happening. I always knew she was alive, I just couldn't prove it. How do you know her?"

"I rather not say just yet. You will know all you need to know once I get the results back, I promise."

"Okay, Drake I'm holding you to your word."

ENVY

CHAPTER TWELVE

Two days later, Drake was at work when he got a phone call. It was the lab letting him know they had the results of the DNA test.

After work, Drake drove over to the lab. He pulled into the parking lot and sat a minute or so before getting out. He was excited to get the results back, but if his suspicion was correct, this may have some bearing on his relationship with Adriane. Drake walked into the lobby of the lab.

"Can I help you, sir?"

"Yes, my name is Drake Stevens, I received a call earlier today that my DNA results were back."

"Okay, let me check on that for you."

The lady walked back with the paperwork in hand. "Well, it looks like you already paid the bill in full." She hands Drake the paper with the results.

"Do you have any questions?"

"No, I'm cool. Thank you."

Drake made his way back to his car, he lay the results on the passenger seat without looking at the result. He pulled out his phone and called Mrs. Brown.

"Hello Drake, how are you?"

"I'm good, Mrs. Brown."

"So, do you have good news for me?"

"I have the results, but I haven't looked at them just yet."

"Drake, what are you waiting for."

"This is going to change some lives, are you ready for that?"

"If it means I will have my daughter back, yes I'm ready for that."

"I'm on my way home, once I get there, I will look at the results and give you a call a little later."

"Okay, Drake." Mrs. Brown said with disappointment in her voice. She wanted to know the results right then.

When Drake finally made it home. He grabbed the paperwork and got out the car. He was walking up to his door when he heard the sound of a car pulling up. He turned around to see Mrs. Brown pulling into his driveway.

Drake shook his head and made his way to her.

"Mrs. Brown, what are you doing here?"

"Drake, I need to know the results right now."

"I can't get into that with you right now," Drake said.

Just then, the front door opened and Adriane walked out. Adriane and Mrs. Brown locked eyes with each other. Adriane doesn't know what, but for some reason, she felt something, as she looked at Mrs. Brown.

Mrs. Brown must have felt the same thing because she slowly made her way to Adriane eyeing her closely.

"Who is this Drake?" Mrs. Brown asked.

Drake is hesitant to answer.

"Drake." Mrs. Brown said as she looked at Drake.

"Who is she?"

"This is my fiancée," Drake said.

"I'm Adriane and you are?"

"I'm Mrs. Brown. I'm Megan's mother."

"What is she doing here Drake?" Adriane asked.

"I don't know Adriane, but I will handle it, go on back inside."

Adriane turned to leave when Drake moved to stand in front of Mrs. Brown.

"You can't be here, right now. I told you I would call you."

"Is she my daughter, Drake?"

Drake sighed.

"Mrs. Brown, please go home. I will come and see you a little later."

"If you don't, just know I will be right back here."

"Okay, okay, I promise I will come and see you right after dinner."

When Drake made it inside, Adriane was standing there with her arms crossed.

"What's going on Drake? Why is Megan's mom coming over here?"

"Megan told her about the fight and she wanted to know what was going on."

"Um… We need to move."

"Why?"

"Because I'm getting a little tired of the fucking Browns." Drake looked at Adriane. He wanted to burst out laughing, but he couldn't because he knew she would be furious.

Drake walked over to Adriane and hugged her. "You need to stop getting so worked up."

"You know I'm so tired of you trying to make it seem like it's just me. How many women do you know that would put up with your ex's bullshit? Now she's got her mother involved."

"I'm going back home and until you can prove to me that your ex and her family will stop coming around, and don't dare call me," Adriane said as she walked down the hall to their bedroom to get some of her things.

Adriane gathered her belongings, walked past Drake without looking at him and walked out the door. She knew that if she looked at him, she would end up staying.

Drake stood in the doorway and watched as Adriane pulled off. He was furious with himself, but Adriane will understand once everything comes out about the Browns.

Drake pulled the paperwork out of his back pocket. He unfolded the paperwork and began reading. Mrs. Brown's DNA is 99.9% a match for Adriane Pruett.

"Damn," Drake said as he tossed the paper on the couch. He walked to the kitchen to the refrigerator and grabbed him a beer. He stood in the kitchen drinking his beer as he looked out the back window.

Adriane pulled up in front of the house. She cuts the engine and got out. She made her way to the front door where she found Mrs. Oliver standing.

"Hey Momma Oliver, how are you?" Adriane asked as she kissed her on the cheek.

"I'm a little tired today. How are you doing?"

"I am so tired of this morning sickness, other than that, I'm good."

"Um hmm, you come on in here and tell me what's really going on."

"Momma Oliver how can you tell when something is bothering me."

"A mother knows honey. So what's going on with you and Drake?"

"I'm tired of his ex- coming around and now her mom showed up today."

"So you're letting his ex and her mom run you away. I never thought of you being a person who would let anyone keep you from what you wanted. I know you love Drake, but if you continue to run from him, someone else will run to him, like Sharon."

Adriane was puzzled. She had no idea that momma Oliver knew anything about Sharon and Drake.

Momma Oliver laughed.

"You see I know way more than you think."

Adriane smiled.

"Drake loves you, make him love you more and more each day that way, it will be very hard for someone to come in between the two of you. And if he does his dirt, you know he's coming home to you."

"What. What are you saying momma Oliver?"

"There is no perfect marriage, but if you love each other, you learn to forgive, you learn to respect each other and stand by one another when the going gets tough. That's what makes a strong marriage. A marriage that can't be easily torn apart. Now you go on back home to Drake and be the strong woman that I raised you to be."

Drake decided to call Mrs. Brown with the news she's been waiting to hear. Drake dialed the number. It rang four times before she picked up.

"Drake, is she my daughter?"

Drake was silent.

"Come on Drake, don't do this to me."

"Yes, Mrs. Brown she's your daughter that you gave birth to 18 years ago."

Just then Drake heard a thump. Mrs. Brown dropped the phone and screamed.

"Thank you, Jesus, thank you!!!" She cried loudly.

Drake ended the call.

Adriane stood at the door with her mouth open. She walked in on Drake telling Mrs. Brown about her daughter.

Adriane cleared her throat, which caused Drake to turn around. Drake almost choked on the beer that was in his mouth.

"Damn, Dri why are you sneaking up on me like that." He asked as he tried to get his thoughts together. He only wondered how much she heard.

"I wasn't trying to sneak up on you. I didn't want to disturb you while you were on the phone. Damn, excuse me for coming back." She said with tears in her eyes.

"Aw baby come here. I didn't mean to snap at you like that."

Adriane started bawling as Drake pulled her close to him.

"Stop crying, please. I don't like to see you cry. Come on over here, we
need to talk about some things."

Adriane and Drake moved to the living room. Drake ran his hand through his hair. He didn't quite know how to break the news to Adriane. He had no idea how she would react to what he was about to tell her.

"You know when you asked me to help you find your birth parents, I thought it would be impossible, but the more you told me what you knew about your birth mom, the more I was able to put two and two together."

"What are you talking about, Drake?"

Drake hesitated.

"I know who your birth parents are?"

"What and how long have you known?"

"I had an idea about a week ago, but I didn't want to say anything until I was for sure. I got the DNA results back today and when you ran out on me, I looked at the results."

Adriane began to put two and two together herself.

"Is Mrs. Brown my birth mother?"

"Yes, she is."

"Is that who you were talking to when I walked in? Why do you look so sad? You act like I'm going to leave or something."

"Do you know what this means, Adriane?"

"Of course I do. It means that bitch is my sister."

"Does this change anything about us?"

"No, not on my part it doesn't."

"Then why the sad face?"

"I thought that when you found out, you would leave me because of what I had with your sister."

"Key word had. That has nothing to do with me. What did Mrs. Brown say when she found out?"

"She cried and thanked Jesus."

Adriane put her hands up to her face. She can't believe this. She had waited her whole life for this day. She thought she would be so happy, but right now, happiness was not what she was feeling.

"So how do you feel about all of this?"

"I don't know. I didn't expect to learn any of this today. I kind of feel numb if that makes any sense."

"I think that's expected. Just take your time and let it soak in. You don't have to meet your family right away. You can do it when you're ready.

Drake got up, walked over to the front door and looked out into the darkness. Life was moving just a little too fast for him right now.

He needed things to slow down so he can enjoy each and every moment of Adriane and her pregnancy.

"Hey babe, are you hungry?"

"Yes, I so hungry I'm about to get sick."

"Well, let's get you something to eat."

"What do you have a taste for?"

"I have a taste for someone who's tall, bowlegged and sexy as hell."

"Oh really. How about you, have him for dessert."

"Sounds good to me."

ENVY

CHAPTER THIRTEEN

The next day at the doctor's office, Drake waited patiently for the nurse to call them back.

"Dang, we have been here for almost an hour and no one has called us back yet."

Adriane looked at Drake with a smile on her face. "You have to be patient."

"I could see if they were packed. We are the only ones here. This is ridiculous."

Twenty minutes later, they were called back. The nurse quickly asked for a sample of urine from Adriane. She wanted to make sure Adriane was actually pregnant. The nurse had Adriane to remove her clothing and she was given a paper gown to put on.

After the examine and the urine sample came back, they were told that Adriane was three weeks pregnant.

Drake could have jumped for joy. "Man, I'm so excited." He said to Adriane. "We need to celebrate."

"I thought we already celebrated."

"Well, I need to celebrate with my boys," Drake said.

Adriane shook her head as she put her clothes back on.

"Can we stop and get food, I'm starving?"

"What do you have in mind?"

"Mexican. Can we go to La Hacienda?"

"You can have whatever you want."

Back at the house, Adriane phoned Mrs. Oliver to thank her for her advice and to give her the due date of her grandchild. She also wanted to talk to her about finding her birth parents, but she decided this should be something that she needed to tell them in person.

"I guess while you're celebrating with your boys, I will go and visit my family and tell them about my birth parents. I just feel it's something that should be told to them in person. I want them to know, that this doesn't change the way I feel about them and that they are still my family, my mother, father, brothers, and sisters."

"I think that's a great idea. Have you decided when you want to meet the Brown's?"

"You know, I not really in a hurry to meet them now. I think meeting Megan the way I did, has left a bad taste in my mouth."

"Just know, the parents are nothing like her."

"Well, she got her personality from someone. Just like I got mine from someone, I wonder who?"

"There's something I need to tell you about your brother."

"Oh, I forgot all about him. What is his name?"

"His name is Michael, but he's in prison?"

"Oh, Jesus!" What did he do?"

"Are you ready for this?"

"Let me take a seat for this."

Adriane took a seat at the kitchen table.

"He murdered six girls."

"Oh my God!. Are you serious?"

This made Adriane think. Now she knows where she gets her craziness from. "I wonder which parent has the killer trait." She said under her breathe.

"What did you say?"

"Oh, nothing. You know, sometimes when you don't know something, about people, sometimes it can be a good thing."

"I guess."

"Last week I knew nothing about my biological family, and now I know that I have a brother who's a serial killer, I have a sister that's a bitch."

Drake laughed. "Well like they say, you can't help what family you're born into."

"That's true, but what I would tell anyone who's searching for family members, just be careful because you never know what you might find out."

"Do I have any other siblings?"

"Yeah you do, but they live in another state. I have never met them, though. I just heard stories about them."

"I'm afraid to even ask about the stories that you've heard."

"Then don't ask," Drake said with a serious look on his face.

"Jesus! Do I even want to know these people?"

"I don't know."

"I should be worried since I'm having a baby with you," Drake said jokingly.

"You're so funny."

"Naw, I'm not worried about anything. My baby will have my traits. And the one good thing is that both of his parents are good looking."

"What do you mean his parents. How do you know it's not a girl? And from what I have learned, the woman is the one that produces the male and the male produces the female. So if we have a son, he will take after his momma."

"Yeah, right."

"I'm serious. Do your research."

"That's not what I have heard."

"Well, you heard wrong," Adriane said as she moved to stand in front of Drake. "You know what Mr. Stevens, I just love you to pieces. There's not another person on this earth, that I would want to father my child."

"Is that so? You mean to tell me that you wouldn't want to have a baby with Pete?"

Adriane moved away from Drake before saying. "Oh, I forgot all about Pete. Hell yeah, I would like to have a baby with him." She said sarcastically as she rolled her eyes at Drake and walked away from him.

"What!"

"See, that's what you get for trying to be funny." She said as she walked quickly down the hall. Drake ran after her.

"Stop Drake," Adriane said laughing.

Drake grabbed hold of her by the waist and pulled her to him. "Now what did you say back there?"

"I said you're the only one I want to have a baby with."

"Yeah, that's what I thought."

"You're such a fucking bully."

"Really," Drake said as he kissed her on the lips.

"Yes, really."

That evening while Drake celebrated with his buddies at Memories Bar & Grill. Adriane pulled up in front of her parents home. She wanted to break the news to them in person about her biological parents.

Adriane got out of the car and made her way up the stairs. John greeted her at the top of the stairs.

"Hey sis, what's going on?"

"Hey John, I am so glad you're here. I have some big news to talk to the family about."

"Is it about the baby?"

"No, but I did go to the doctor today and I now know my due date."

"So when is my niece or nephew due?"

"April 15."

"You're joking, right?"

"No, I'm serious.'

"On my birthday. That is so cool."

"I figured you would get a kick out of that."

Adriane and John make their way inside, where they found everyone sitting in the den.

"Hey everyone," Adriane said as she gave Momma & Papa Oliver a kiss.

"Girl you got us on pins and needles wondering what you're going to tell us." Papa Oliver said.

Adriane took a seat next to Momma Oliver and grabbed a hold of her hand.

"Well, you guys know I have always been interested in finding my biological parents since I got here. So last week, Drake and I went to the library to see if we could find anything in the archive file for a death certificate or something. But in the meantime, I told Drake what I knew about my family and he just happened to remember something about a family that he knew. He knew that they had lost their daughter at birth and that she was a triplet. She also had the same first name as my birth mom. He went and purchased a DNA kit and swabbed my mouth while I was asleep. He didn't want me to get my hopes up so he kept it from me, but the person who he thought was my mom, he talked with her about it and convinced her to take the DNA test. Well, it came back the other day as a match. Deloris Brown is my biological mother and Megan, Drake's ex-girlfriend is my sister."

"Are you serious?" John asked.

"I know, it's crazy."

"But what I want you guys to know, is that I still consider you guys my family. You're the only family that I have known. No one will ever take your place."

Adriane looked at Momma Oliver, who has tears in her eyes.

"What's wrong, Momma Oliver? Don't cry." Adriane said as she wiped Momma Oliver's face.

Papa Oliver pulled his wife to him. "Sweetheart, it's okay, you're not losing a daughter.

"I know, but everything is happening so fast. First, she moved out, then we find out she's pregnant, then she gets engaged and now, she has a new family."

"No, I don't have a new family. What I have is an addition to my family. I told you guys, you will always be my family no matter what."

"How does Drake feel about it?" Marie asked.

"He hasn't really said. He was more concerned about the baby. Right now he's out celebrating with his boys."

"So are you happy that you found your parents?" Momma Oliver asked.

"To be honest, No, I'm not. I have had several run ends with Megan, so I can't stand her and then I found out that my brother Michael is in prison for murdering six girls. And then Drake tells me about my other siblings who live out of state. He said they're bad news as well."

"So have you met your mother and father yet?"

"No, I am not ready for that just yet. I'm not sure I will ever be ready to meet them."

"You have to at least meet them and learn more about them, at least you'll know where you come from," John said.

"I guess, but just not right now."

Denise Hill

CHAPTER FOURTEEN

Adriane was laying in bed when she heard noises. She looked around the room trying to figure out where the noise was coming from when she realized it was coming from outside, outside her bedroom window.

Adriane called out to Drake, but he doesn't respond. Adriane lay back down, she thought it was Drake messing around outside, but when she continued to hear the noise, she got up and made her way into the living room. She looked around for Drake, but he was nowhere in sight. She went to look out the window to see if she saw his car, but she didn't. Now, fear set in. Adriane went into the kitchen and grabbed a knife and made her way out onto the porch.

"Who's there?" She called out as she stepped off the porch and headed around to the side of the house. The noise stopped and so did Adriane. She stood there not knowing what to do next when out of nowhere someone hit her in the head with a crowbar knocking her to the ground.

Drake pulled up and made his way to the porch. He rubbed his head wondering why the front door was open this late at night. Drake walked into the house, the lights were all on, but Adriane was nowhere to be found.

"Adriane, where are you?" Drake yelled from the kitchen. Drake headed back to the bedroom to look for Adriane. He checked the bathroom and then he went back outside to the porch and called out to her.

"Adriane, baby where are you?"

He walked over to her car, the car doors were locked. He turned around when he heard movement in the bushes on the side of the house. He made his way over to where he saw Adriane trying to get up off the ground.

"What are you doing?" He asked as he helped her up off the ground and at this point, he sees the gash and blood on her forehead.

"Drake, someone hit me," Adriane said just before passing out again in his arms.

Drake carried Adriane into the house and laid her on the couch and called the paramedics.

Hours later, Adriane awoke in the hospital. When she opened her eyes, she sees Drake, two white male police officers, and her family.

"Hey, sweet pea." Mrs. Oliver said as she rubbed Adriane's hand.

"You gave us a scare, young lady." Mr. Oliver said

"Hey babe, how do you feel?"

"What happened," Adriane asked as she felt her head.

"That's what we want to ask you." The officer said as he walked up to her bed.

"Do you remember anything about last night?

"I remember very little."

"Why were you outside the house?" The other officer asked.

"I heard some noise outside the bedroom window. At first, I thought it was Drake so I ignored it, but then it continued and when I didn't see his car out front, I decided to go out to see where the noise was coming from. That's all I remember."

"You told me that someone hit you," Drake said.

"I'm sorry, right now I don't remember anything else."

"Don't be sorry," Drake said. I'm just glad you and the baby are okay."

"When can I go home?"

"I'll have to check with your doctor," Drake said.

"I have just one more question for you." The officer said. "Do you know of anyone that would want to hurt you?"

Adriane laughed. "Yeah, I could think of a few people."

"Can we get those names?"

"Megan Brown, Sharon Tate, and Pete Jefferson."

"And why would these people want to harm you?"

"I used to date the women and Pete tried to attack her a couple of weeks ago."

"Oh my God! Adriane, why didn't you tell us about Pete?"

"Mom, it wasn't a big deal."

"Personally, I don't believe it was Pete. He's not that stupid."

"Do you have their addresses?"

Adriane gave them the addresses for Sharon and Pete. "I don't have Megan's address." Adriane doesn't want them talking to Megan just yet.

The next day, Adriane was lying on the couch in the living room watching TV when someone knocked on the front door.

"I'll get it," Drake yelled from the kitchen.

Drake opened the door to find Sharon standing there.

"How dare that bitch of yours send the police over to my house questioning me about being over here and hitting her. It wasn't me, but now I wish it had been me. That bitch got what she deserved."

Adriane got up off the couch and went to the door. Drake stood in her way so she can't get out.

"Don't let me find out it was you bitch because I will fuck your ass up. Trust and believe that."

"Blah, blah, blah. That's all you do is talk."

"Was I talking last month when I beat that ass?"

"Sharon, get off of my property," Drake said as he shut the door and looked at Adriane.

"There you go again."

"Drake, I don't know who you think I am, but I am not about to be quiet while these bitches come over here. Now what I didn't do was try to go at her. Give me credit for that." She said as she rolled her eyes at Drake and walked back over to the couch.

Twenty minutes later, Drake called Adriane for dinner.

"I'm not hungry." She said, knowing darn well, she was starving, but she was just pissed at him.

"You know you need to eat something Adriane," Drake fixed her plate and took it to her in the living room. He knew she was hungry.

Ten minutes later, Drake walked back into the living room and found Adriane's plate clean. He laughed to himself as he looked at her.

"Who inhaled your food since you were not hungry?" Adriane rolled her eyes. Drake took her plate back to the kitchen and laughed out loud just to piss her off.

"Oh, he makes me so sick." She said

"Do I really?" Drake asked as he stood in the entryway of the kitchen and living room.

"I'm sorry Dri, but I'm only looking out for you. You always let people take you there. You need to learn to control your temper or your temper just might get you in trouble and where will that leave me and the baby?"

"Like I said, I will not let anyone, just talk shit to me. I have a right to defend myself whether it's verbally or physically."

Later that evening, Drake got a call.

"Hello."

"Good evening Drake. How are you?"

"I'm good, Mrs. Brown. How are you?"

"I would be better if I could see my daughter."

"Well, that's not up to me. That's Adriane's decision and right now, she's not ready."

"But I'm her mother."

"Mrs. Brown, can you hold on for a minute?"

Drake walked over to Adriane. "Can you at least talk to her?" Adriane looked at him like he's crazy. "Do I look like I want to talk to her right now?"

"Adriane, she's your mother."

"And when I'm ready I will reach out to her."

Drake shook his head and walked back into the kitchen.

"Mrs. Brown, like I said before, she will reach out to you when she's ready." Mrs. Brown disconnected the call. She was furious that Adriane wouldn't talk to her.

"What is her problem? It's not like I gave her up." Mrs. Brown told her husband.

"Honey, I don't think this has anything to do you with us, I think it's more about Megan and Drake."

Megan stood in the hallway listening to her parents. No one had any idea that Megan knew Adriane was her sister. When Megan first learned of this, she was so angry with her parents, Adriane and Drake. She saw how happy her parents were when they learned that she was alive. She was envious of Adriane. Adriane had everything. She had Drake, she's carrying his baby and is engaged to him. She has two families now. Megan felt so alone and has been since her brother went to prison. He was the only one who she felt really cared about her.

Megan stormed out the house. She got in her car and drove around for hours. "I hate my life." She screamed as she hit the steering wheel.

Two hours later, Megan found herself down the street from Drake's. She sat in her car watching the house. She watched as Drake walked out onto the porch with a beer in his hand. Megan pulled out her phone and dialed Drake's number. Drake picked up on the second ring.

"Hello, Megan."

"Hey, Drake. How are you?"

"I'm good. What can I do for you, Megan?"

Megan laughed.

"Do you have to ask?"

"Yes, I do."

"Can you meet me somewhere?"

"Right now?"

"No silly. Friday after work."

"Where and why?"

"At my parent's rental property. I have something there that I want you and Adriane to have."

"Is that all?"

"Yes. I will see you there at 6 pm and don't be late." Megan said as she disconnected the call.

"See I know he still loves me." She said out loud.

Friday rolled around and Megan had everything set up for her and Drake. She called him just to make sure he was still coming.

"Megan I told you I would be there."

"Okay, I just wanted to make sure."

Megan just finished taking the steaks off the grill when she sees Drake pulling up.

She sat the steaks on the table and made her way to the front door.

"Hey, babe," Megan said as she pulled Drake inside

Drake looked puzzled as he looked around the room.

"What's going on Megan?"

"What do you mean?"

"You know damn well what I mean. I thought you had something for me and Adriane."

"Oh, I do, but first, you have to have dinner with me."

"Dinner, Megan really."

"I know you are starving. I know how you are when you get off work. So come on in here and have dinner and a little wine with me."

"Okay, and then I will have to be on my way."

Drake and Megan sat at the table having dinner and drinking wine when she broke the news to him about her miscarriage.

"So it looks like you're off the hook."

"That's good to know since Adriane is expecting."

"When's her due date?"

"April 15th."

"Um… Would you like some more wine?"

"Just a little and then I have to go."

"Why are you in such a hurry Drake? What's wrong with friends having dinner together and from what I hear, we will be more than just friends."

Drake looked over at Megan. "What are you saying, Megan."

"I know Adriane is my sister."

"So how do you feel about that?"

"I'm not sure right now. Ask me a little later." Megan said as she laughed.

Two hours later, Drake and Megan had moved to the outside on the deck. Drake, who was feeling a little light headed after having three glasses of wine. Drake decided he should get going. He checked his watch and was taken back by the time.

"Oh my God! Adriane is going to kill me."

"What, so she has you on a schedule?"

"Now you know me better than that. No one controls me."

"Well, come on, let's go inside so I can give you your gift."

Drake followed Megan inside the house and waited for her to bring the gift she had for him and Megan, but when she took a little too long, he climbed the stairs to the bedroom where he found her in a pink and black lace lingerie.

Megan looked up when she saw Drake. "You like?"

Drake had to admit, she looked damn good and the color against her caramel skin did wonders for her.

"Megan, don't do this."

"Do what?" She said as she walked towards him.

"I thought you said you had something for me."

"This is for you." She said as she pointed to her body.

Denise Hill

CHAPTER FIFTEEN

The next morning, Drake awoke just as the sun was coming up. He scanned the room trying to adjust his eyes. He didn't know where he was until he looked beside him and sees Megan.

"Oh shit!" Drake said as he jumped up from the bed.

"What the fuck happened?"

Megan stirred awake.

"What's wrong? Where are you going?"

Drake paced back and forth.

"What did you put in my wine last night?"

"Oh, don't you dare blame this on me. You wanted me just as much as I wanted you. No one forced you to make love to me all night."

"Man, I can't believe this shit. What am I going to tell Adriane?"

"If it will make you feel any better, lie to her, but you and I both know what happened last night," Megan said as she laughed.

Drake put his clothes on and left out in a hurry.

"What am I going to tell Adriane? If I tell her the truth, I know she will leave me and I can't have that."

Adriane was up all night calling Drake, but all of her calls went straight to voicemail. She called all the hospitals she even called to see if he had been arrested.

Adriane had fallen asleep in the living room on the couch as she cried herself to sleep. She had no idea what was going on, she only hoped and prayed that Drake was safe.

Adriane was awakened when she heard the sound of a car pulling up.

Adriane jumped up and peered through the curtain to see Drake's truck.

Drake pulled up and cut the engine. He sat for a minute or so, afraid to go inside. He had no idea what was in store for him when he entered.

Drake got out and walked slowly to the house. He inserted his key into the lock, turned the knob and opened the door to find Adriane sitting on the couch.

"Good morning"

"Good morning." She said calmly.

"I'm so glad you're safe. I had no idea what happened to you last night.

I just don't understand how you feel staying out all night is acceptable." Adriane said as she stood up.

"I'm sorry Dri. I didn't plan on staying out all night, but I had too much to drink, so I decided to crash at Mike's."

"That's good you have enough sense not to drive, but why didn't you call and let me know what was going on?"

"Too much to drink," Drake said as he moved to hug Adriane.

"Oh my God! Adriane yelled as the tears begin to fall.

"You smell like sex you son of a bitch." She said as she slapped the living daylight out of Drake.

Drake was stunned by the slap. Drake grabbed her by the shoulders and moved her backward up against the wall.

"Don't you ever as long as you live, raise your hand to strike me again. Do I make myself clear?'

"Fuck you, Drake! You didn't even have enough sense to shower before coming home. You have no respect for me at all." Adriane said as she broke free of Drake and made her way down the hall to the bathroom.

In the meantime, Drake phone rang. He looked at the number and sees it was Megan.

"What do you want?"

"Damn, it that how you address someone you just spent making love to all night? I just wanted to make sure everything's good on the home front."

"Does it matter to you?"

"No, not really. I'm just lying here in bed watching our sex tape thinking of you."

"Oh God!" Drake said.

"Don't worry your precious Adriane will never know anything about this tape as long as you do what I ask of you?"

"And how can I make that tape disappear?"

"You can't, but you can make sure she will never see it."

"How is that?"

"Just do as I say."

"What do you want from me?

"Nothing right now, but I will call you later and let you know when and where we can meet to finish what we started last night," Megan said before she disconnected the call.

"Man, what have I gotten myself into?" He said as he flopped down in the chair.

Adriane sat in the bathroom on the toilet bawling her eyes out. "Why God! Why do bad things continue to happen to me? I try to

be a good person, but it doesn't matter, bad things still happen. Why did you even allow me to be born, why?" She cried. Adriane was in the bathroom for about thirty minutes before she heard a knock at the door.

"Adriane baby, are you okay?"

"Leave me alone."

"Adriane, don't be like that. We need to sit down and talk." Just then, the bathroom door swung open.

"Talk, talk about what? What could you possibly say that's going to make me feel any better about you sleeping with someone? Huh, you tell me, Drake?'

"It's not what you think. Let's just sit down and talk." "Right now I don't have anything to say to you and I don't have time to listen to any of your bullshit. So talk to your damn self." Adriane said as she slammed the door in Drake's face.

"I'm not leaving until you come out. You have to come out at some point and when you do, I will be right here."

"Suit yourself."

Drake took a seat outside the bathroom on the floor waiting for Adriane to come out."

An hour passed, Adriane was still locked inside.

"Adriane I know you're hungry. You have to feed my baby. Let's go to brunch. We don't have to talk right now if you don't want to."

Two minutes later, the door opened slightly. I need something to eat, but I am not in the mood to be around people so can you bring something back."

"Sure, what do you want?"

While Drake was getting breakfast, Adriane took a shower. When she was finished, she reached for the towel that she placed on the counter before stepping out, but it wasn't there.

"What the f..." She said as she looked around for the towel. "Now I know I am not losing my mind. I placed a towel right here on the counter." She said out loud as she continued to look for it.

When Drake returned, the first thing that caught his eyes was the white bath towel laying on the couch in the living room. He made his way to the kitchen where he placed the food and went back to the living room to take the towel to the bathroom. When he lifted the towel, he was stunned to find what was underneath it. It was the pink and black lingerie that Megan had on last night.

Just then panic set in. Drake rushed to the kitchen and put the lingerie into the trash can and then he called out to Adriane.

"Adriane, are you okay?" He asked as he rushed down the hall to the bathroom.

Adriane was in the bedroom putting her clothes on when she heard Drake. Adriane stepped out into the hall.

"What's wrong with you?"

"Oh my God! You're okay?"

"And why wouldn't I be."

"Did you leave this towel in the living room?"

"No, I was looking for that towel. I laid this on the bathroom counter, but when I finished showering it wasn't there."

The look of terror showed on Drake's face.

"Drake, what is going on? You look like you just saw a ghost?"

"I'm cool. Come on so you can eat." Drake said, trying to sound calm, but he knew if he didn't come clean with Adriane about Megan, he just might lose Adriane for good.

As the two were sitting at the kitchen table eating, they heard a knock at the door.

"I'll get it," Drake said.

Drake took his time getting the door and when he opened the door, there was no one there. Drake stepped out onto the porch and stepped on something on the ground. Drake looked down and moved his foot and sees a card.

He bent down, picked up the card and opened the envelope. He pulled the card out and read the inscription.

Drake sweetheart,

Thank you so much for last night. The lovemaking was out of this world. I can't wait for part two!!!!!

Megan....

Drake looked around to see if he saw Megan anywhere in sight. Megan sat in her car and watched as Drake looked around.

"Poor baby, you haven't experienced anything yet."

Drake walked over to the side of the porch looking out for any signs of Megan, and when he realized she had left, he folded the card, put it in his pocket and made his way back inside.

"Who was it?"

"Nobody?"

"What do you mean nobody? I heard someone knocking."

"When I got to the door, no one was there."

"Drake, what's going on? I'm starting to feel unsafe here."

"You're safe, don't worry."

Tears started to roll down Adriane's face. Drake looked up at her and moved to her side.

"Adriane, baby, please don't cry. I love you more than anything and I will never do anything intentionally to hurt you and I will not let anyone else hurt you. Please tell me you believe that."

"You won't let anyone else hurt me. Sorry boo, but you already let that happened while you were out celebrating with your boys and I got hit in the head. I feel like I'm getting hurt all the way around dealing with you."

"Dang, you sure know how to hurt a brother."

"I'm just telling you the truth."

"I promise Adriane, things will get better."

"Um… I'm going to hold you to that promise."

"I need to know something, and I need for you to be honest. Were you with Megan last night?"

Drake thought about it, if I'm honest, she will leave and if I'm not and she finds out and then she will leave.

Adriane looked at Drake.

"There's no need for you to answer. I already have my answer."

"What are you talking about?"

"You just told me what I wanted to know without you even saying anything. If it takes you too long to answer a question, it's because you don't want, to tell the truth, but that's okay. I got something for that ass."

Adriane said as she placed her napkin on her plate and moved away from the kitchen table.

Adriane turned around to let at Drake.

"Remember sweetheart, payback is a motherfucking bitch."

ENVY

CHAPTER SIXTEEN

The next day, Adriane called Pete and asked him to meet her at Panera.

Pete was thrilled to get the call from Adriane, but he was a little leery about meeting her.

"What's going on Adriane?" Pete asked.

"Nothing Pete, I just want to talk to you?"

"Where's your boy?"

"Don't worry about him, we are no longer together." Adriane lied.

Adriane and Pete agree to meet at 3 pm for a late lunch.

Drake sat in the living room and listened while Adriane was on the phone. He knew she was meeting someone, but he didn't know who.

Adriane was in the bedroom getting dressed when Drake walked in.

"Who are you meeting?"

"A friend, why?"

"Is it a female or male?"

"Right now, I don't think you have the right to even ask me that."

"Oh, really?"

"That's right. You fucked a bitch, plus you spent the night with her so the way I see things, you are going to get just what you deserve."

"Alright, don't let me catch you doing anything."

"Please don't threaten me."

"I'm just saying."

"And I'm just saying. Why don't you go and be with that bitch you were with last night and leave me the fuck alone."

"Well, if you feel like that. Why in the hell are you still here with me?"

"Oh, I won't be for long."

Drake grabbed a hold of Adriane's arm.

"Let me tell you something. I will never let you go, especially since you're carrying my seed."

"I can still do something about that, believe me, it's not too late," Adriane said as she broke free from Drake's grip.

"You better be damn glad I was taught to never put my hands on a woman, because if I wasn't, I would beat your ass real good."

"Yeah, and I would kill you in your fucking sleep too."
Drake laughed and walked away. Just remember what I said."

"Yeah, yeah, yeah."

Later that afternoon, while Adriane was meeting with Pete, Drake got a call from Megan.

"Where's my bitch ass sister?"

"Out, Why, do you want to talk to her?"
Hell naw, I need for you to meet me at the rental in 30 minutes."

"Megan, what is it that you want?"

"Do you have to ask? I want the D," Megan said before hanging up.

"Jesus, what am I going to do?" Drake said as he leaned up against the living room wall.
Drake made his way down the hall and into the bathroom. He removed his clothes, turned on the shower and got in.
Twenty minutes later, he was on his way to the rental home to meet Megan.
Drake has no idea that Megan was trying to get pregnant. She had lied to him about being pregnant just to get back with him and was hoping to get pregnant, but what she didn't count on was Adriane being in the picture.
Drake pulled into the driveway as he sees Megan sitting on the front deck waiting for him. She had wine, food, and a hot wet juicy pussy just for him.
Drake got out of the car and made his way to her.

"Megan we need to talk."

"No, we need to eat, drink and make passionate love. That's what we need to do. There's no need for talking."

"I don't know what you're up to, but you can count me out."

"Oh really, how would Adriane feel about this?" She handed Drake her phone and allowed him to watch them having sex last night

"So this is what you've stooped to, blackmailing people?"

"No, just you, so have a seat so we can get started."

"I don't think I want any part of this. If you're going to tell Adriane, then go right ahead and if I lose her, just know, I will not be getting back with you? And another thing, don't come to my home anymore or I will get the police involved.

Adriane and Pete sat at Panera talking.

"I just wanted to apologize to you for what happened between you and Drake."

"No, I need to apologize to you for trying to force myself on you."

"How have you been, Pete?"

"I'm good and you?"

"I'm okay, I guess."

"What do you mean you guess?"

"I'm pregnant and Drake's cheating on me."

"Oh, congratulations, I guess, and how do you know he's cheating?"

"Thanks, I guess. Drake stayed out all night last night and comes home this morning smelling like sex and when I asked him if he was with someone last night, it took him too long to answer."

"Adriane, I'm sorry, but if you give me another chance, I promise you will not have any regrets and I don't care that you're pregnant by another man. I will accept this child as my own."

Tears begin to well up in Adriane's eyes.

"Pete, that's so sweet of you, but you don't know what you're getting yourself into? How would you support us?"

"I'm going to college in state at night and I will work for my dad during the day."

"I'm planning on going to school as well, pregnant and all."

"My dad owns a lot of real estate in Indy and I know he will give us a house so we won't have to worry about paying a mortgage. Just think about it, Adriane."

"I will." She said as she kissed Pete on the lips. Adriane was just trying to have some fun and to get back at Drake for sleeping around.

Adriane and Pete eat and continued to talk. Drake pulled up and spotted Adriane's car. He rode around the parking lot looking to see if he could see her inside and when he did, his heart stopped for a second.

"What the fuck." He said as he saw Adriane and Pete together.

Pete and Adriane continued to sit and talk after they finished eating.

Drake pulled out his phone and called Adriane. Adriane pulled her phone out of her purse and saw it was Drake calling so she let it go to voice mail.

"Damn," Drake said as he hit the steering wheel.

Drake got out of the car and sat on the hood and waited for Adriane and Pete to come out.

Megan called Drake as he sat and waited for Adriane and Pete to come out. Drake looked at the number and deleted the call. Megan called back and he deleted the call again, so she sent him a text message.

"Drake, you think I'm playing, just wait until you get home."

"Whatever," Drake replied back.

Just then, Adriane and Pete walked out of Panera. Pete walked Adriane to her car and they kissed.

Drake almost had a heart attack.

"Aw shit, Pete's ass is dead," Drake said as he hopped in his car. He waited for Adriane to pull off and then he followed her. He stayed two cars behind her so she didn't see him.

When Adriane made it home, Drake waited a couple of minutes before pulling in.

Adriane walked up the stairs and found a note taped to the front door.

"What is this?" She asked out loud.

Just then, Drake pulled up and sees Adriane reading something and then he remembered what Megan said.

Drake hopped out of the car and ran up to Adriane.

"What is that?" He asked.

"Dang, what's wrong with you running up here like a bat out of hell."

Adriane unlocked the door and walked in. "Well, what does the note say?"

"It doesn't say anything. It has a YouTube link."

Drake almost shit his pants. "Can I see that?"

"Wait. Let me put this link into my phone and then you can see it.

"Drake grabbed the note out of Adriane's hand before she can enter it into her phone.

"Man, what is wrong with you?"

Drake goes into the bathroom and pulled his phone out and pulled up YouTube and keyed the link in. He was shocked to sce that Megan had put the sex tape out on YouTube and it already had 1000 views.

Adriane stood at the bathroom door waiting for Drake to come out so she can get the note from him.

When Drake came out, he had a sad look on his face.

"Who died?"

"What?"

"You look like someone has died."

"We need to talk Adriane and we need to talk right now."

Drake guided Adriane outside to the porch. Adriane sat on the top step as Drake stood.

"Who did you have lunch with today?"

"A friend."

"A male or female?"

"A female."

"Don't you dare lie to me, Adriane."

"Well, if you don't believe me, why don't you tell me who I had lunch with?"

"Pete."

Adriane looked up at Drake in disbelief.

"Did you follow me? You have a lot of nerves after the shit you pulled."

"We are not talking about me, we are talking about you?"

"Like hell, we are. I didn't sleep with anyone, but you did. So what if I had lunch with Pete, I didn't fuck him. Can you say you didn't fuck who you spent the night with?"

Drake was speechless.

"Now give me the note."

Drake tore the note into tiny pieces and threw it at her.

"You're such an ass."

Drake walked back into the house and back into the bathroom where he called Megan.

"Megan if you don't take the video down, I will see you in court."

"I guess I'll just see you in court." She said as she ended the call.

Adriane was still sitting outside on the porch trying to figure out what was going on with Drake. He's acting like a totally different person Adriane continued to sit when her phone rang. She saw it was Renee.

"Hey Renee what's going on?"

"Adriane, have you seen the video?"

"What video?"

"Go to YouTube and type in Me and My baby daddy."

Adriane pulled up YouTube and typed it in and pushed the play button.

"Do you have it up yet?"

"I'm waiting for the commercial to finish playing. Okay, I just hit the skip button."

Adriane watched and recognized Megan, but when she sees Drake, she was floored. Now she knows who he spent the night with.

"Renee let me call you back. I have a nigga to kill."

"No, Adriane, don't do anything you will regret. Get in your car and come see me, now."

No Renee, I can't do that." Adriane said as she ended the call. Renee didn't know what to do or who she should call, so she called John.

Adriane walked in the house just as Drake was coming out of the bathroom.

"Are you still seeing Megan?"

"What are you talking about?"

"Don't play with me Drake. Tell me the truth." Adriane said as calmly as she could be. She was so calm that she actually frightened Drake.

Drake stood not knowing if he should come clean or not.

"Adriane I don't have time for this."

"But you got time for this, don't you," She said as she held up the video so he could see.

Adriane dropped the phone, charged at Drake and before he can do anything she was upon him, beating him in the face.

"You fucking whore. How dare you humiliate me like this? Why did I have to find out like this? I should kill you dead right now."

"I'm sorry baby, I am sorry," Drake said as he grabbed Adriane and held her to keep her from hitting him. I wanted to tell you, but I didn't know how. I was afraid I would lose you."

"Well, guess what, you will have another man raising your child, bitch."

"Don't you do that to me, Adriane, I will kill you."

Adriane bawled her fist up and hit Drake in his eye. Drake stumbled back and Adriane took off running down the hall with Drake on her trail.

"I told you before about hitting me. Didn't I?" Drake said as he ran after her. Adriane was almost out the door when she ran into John. John stepped in front of Adriane and stared at Drake.

"I wish you would put your fucking hands on her."

"John, you know I would never hit her. I just want to talk to her."

"Not right now you won't. John turned around to Adriane. "Go get some clothes. You're coming home for a while."
Adriane moved past Drake as the tears rolled down his face.

"Please Adriane, don't leave me. I love you."

"Is that why you slept with Megan?" John asked.

"John, she drugged me, man, I swear. It had to have been in the wine she gave me."

"Why were you even with her?"

"She told me to meet her at her parent's rental home. She said she had a gift for Adriane and me, but when I get there, she had dinner and wine. I ate and had some wine and that's all I remember."

"Why didn't you come and talk to Adriane about this? You let her and all her friends see this. How do you think this makes her feel?"

"I know, I am so sorry. I just need for Adriane to understand and believe me."

"That's not going to happen tonight. Maybe tomorrow or the next day."
Adriane walked out with a duffle bag. Drake walked over to her.

"Adriane please talk to me. Don't leave me, baby, please, don't leave." Drake cried.
Adriane walked out the door with John on her trail. Drake followed behind them and stood on the porch and watched as they both pulled off.

Denise Hill

CHAPTER SEVENTEEN

Drake sat on the porch drinking the entire night. He couldn't believe he just lost everything. "How could I have been so stupid to go to Megan's that evening in the first place?" He asked himself.

Drake pulled out his phone and dialed Adriane's number. The call goes straight to voicemail. He tried to reach Adriane several times after that, but all his calls went to voicemail. He didn't blame her for being upset because he was upset that he saw her and Pete kissing.

Adriane lay in her old bed tossing and turning. She couldn't believe Drake would do this to her. She truly believed in her heart that Megan set this up, but she will never forgive Drake for even being with her. And if Megan did put something in his drink, if he had not been with her, then none of this would have happened. Sometimes you have to use common sense when it comes to dealing with an ex who still has feelings, for you. And if they're your ex, it just means they are in your past and that's where they need to stay, in your past.

The next day while Drake was at work, Adriane went over to the house to get more of her belonging, but when she got there and unlocked the front door, and walked in to see Megan sitting at the kitchen table eating.

"What the fuck are you doing here?" Adriane asked as she walked further into the house and sees Megan eating food that she bought.

"Hey sis, how are you? Drake invited me over last night."

"Like hell, he did. And why are you eating my food?" Adriane said as she walked over and knocked the bowl of soup on the floor.

"You know what, I'm so sorry that I share the same DNA as you."

"Adriane you have such a childish behavior."

"Bitch if you don't get out of her I'm going to have a killer's behavior like our brother."
Megan slowly got up from the table and walked to stand in front of Adriane. "Don't you fucking dare say a word about my brother you know nothing about him you dumb bitch." Megan stood there with her nostrils flaring ready to fight.

"Like I said, if you don't get out of here you will be buried six feet under and if you think I'm playing, try me."

"Adriane, can you do me a favor and tell Drake that I really enjoyed last night," Megan said as she walked out the door. Adriane charged after Megan.

"Keep on Megan you're going to get what you're asking for."
Adriane said as she stood out on the porch and watched as Megan backed out of the driveway.

Adriane was so angry that she called Drake, but her call went to voicemail. So she decided to pay him a visit at his business. Adriane locked the front door and made her way to her car. She sat for a minute before backing out trying to calm her nerves. She didn't want to cause a scene with Drake so she had to be calm when she arrived.

Fifteen minutes later, Adriane pulled into the parking lot of DS Productions.

She walked in and sees the receptionist sitting behind her desk. She walked over to her giving her the eye. Drake never mentioned that he had a female receptionist who looked like she just stepped off a magazine cover. Adriane thought to herself.

"Hello, how are you?" Adriane said.

"I'm good and you?" The receptionist said.

"I'm here to see Drake," Adriane said.

"And you are?"

"Adriane, his fiancée."

"Oh, It's nice to finally meet you. I have heard a lot about you."

"Um... I bet." Adriane said as she smiled at the receptionist.

"Let me see if Drake's available." She said as she walked down the hall to Drake's office.

The receptionist knocks at Drake's door.

"Come in."

"Drake, your fiancée is out front to see you."

Drake looked puzzled.

"Can you send her back?"

"Sure."

Bailey walked back to the lobby. "Adriane, can you follow me."

Adriane followed behind Bailey. Now she felt a little intimidated and self- conscious.

"Why would Drake want me when he could have Bailey?" Adriane thought. She wondered if Drake had ever dated Bailey.

Bailey stopped open Drake's door and stood to the side so Adriane can enter.

"Thank you, Bailey," Drake said.

Drake got up from behind his desk and walked over to Adriane to give her a hug.

Adriane took a step back.

"We're not like that right now. I only came here because you didn't answer my call. I went to the house to get the rest of my belongings and who did I see sitting at the kitchen table eating?"

"What. What are you talking about?"

"Megan was in the house. She told me to tell you that she really enjoyed last night. She said you called her over to spend the night."

"Oh, that's some bullshit. I don't know what Megan is trying to pull, but that never happened. I was at home last night by my damn self."

"Adriane, why would you bring this nonsense to my business?"

"Drake, I tried calling you, but you didn't answer."

"Well, whatever happens in my personal life should never be brought to my business so if you don't have anything else to say to me, I think you should leave."

"Oh, so it's like that now?"

"Yeah, I won't discuss anything with you here unless it's about business. If you want to talk, meet me at the house later."

Adriane looked at Drake with sadness in her eyes. She sees the bruise under his eye that she caused by hitting him.

Adriane walked out before the tears begin to fall. Drake followed behind her.

"Adriane," Drake called out to her, but Adriane kept walking. She walked out the door and to her car without looking back.

Megan sat parked across the street and watched as Adriane pulled off. Megan pulled into the parking lot, cut the engine and got out. She walked inside and greeted Bailey.

"Hey, Bailey is Drake available?"

Bailey looked surprised to see Megan. She knew Drake and Megan had been broken up for months.

"Um… let me check."

Bailey walked quickly back to Drake's office. She knocked at the door before opening and going inside.

"Drake, Megan is out front to see you."

"Tell her I'm busy."

Bailey walked back to the lobby where Megan stood.

"Megan, I'm sorry, but Drake's busy."

"Right," Megan said as she turned to leave, but decided to walk back to Drake's office.

"Megan!" Bailey called out.

Megan walked in on Drake as he stood looking out his office window.

"Megan what the hell do you want?"

"I wanted to talk with you."

"So why didn't you call?"

"Because I know you wouldn't answer."

Drake shook his head. His day was getting better by the minute.

"I don't think you and I have anything to talk about. You put the video out, Adriane saw it, so there's nothing else you can do to me."

"I'm sorry Drake. I just want you back and I will do whatever it takes to get you back.'

"There's nothing you can do now since you put that video out. Now I see what type of person you are and I want nothing to do with you. You are a very envious person."

"Well, just remember who's DNA your precious Adriane has," Megan said as she walked out.

"Damn, what is it with those Brown women," Drake said to himself.

When Drake arrived home, he found soup and a bowl on his kitchen floor. He cleaned the mess up, grabbed a beer out of the refrigerator and sat out on the porch.
Drake pulled his phone out and called Adriane to see if she wanted to talk. He let the phone ring five times before hanging up.

"I guess she doesn't want to talk."
Drake continued to sit and drink his beer when he heard a noise around the side of the house. Drake got up and moved to the side of the porch when he saw Pete walking up.

"Aw ain't this a bitch. You know I should beat your fucking ass for kissing my girl."
"I didn't come here to fight. I came here to verify that you and Adriane were no longer together."

"And who told you that?"
She did yesterday when we had dinner."

"Oh, really. Well, I guess since she told you that, then it's true."

"I just wanted you to know that I will take damn good care of your child. I will raise it likes it's my own."

Why did Pete say that? Drake jumped off the porch and
before Pete knew what was going on, Drake was beating his
ass. Pete didn't have a chance with Drake so he pulled out his
gun and fired it at Drake hitting him in the shoulder.
Pete took off running as Drake, fell to the ground.

"Aw shit," Drake said as the pain hit him.
Drake grabbed his phone and dialed 911.

    Later that evening, Adriane was sitting in the kitchen
talking to Renee when she got a call from an unknown
number. She decided to let it go to voicemail, but something
told her to answer it.

"Hello."

"Is this Adriane Pruett?"

"Yes, it is."

"This is Sarah from Community North Hospital. I'm calling
you because you are listed as a relative to a Drake Stevens."

"Drake, has something happened to him?"

"Yes, he has been shot."

"Shot!" Adriane screamed. "I'm on my way."
Adriane got off the phone and by now, the family was standing
in the kitchen.

"Adriane what happened?"

"It's Drake, he's been shot."

ENVY

CHAPTER EIGHTEEN

By the time Adriane and Renee make it to the hospital, Drake was being transferred to a room for the night. Renee sat out in the lobby as Adriane went back to see Drake. Adriane walked into the room and found Drake asleep. She walked over to him, bent down and kissed him on the lips. Drake opened his eyes and smiled when he saw it was Adriane.

"Aw, so you do care?"

"You know damn well I care about you," Adriane said as she rubbed her hand across his face.

"To be honest, I didn't think you would come." Adriane grabbed hold of Drake's hand and held it against her chest.

"What happened, Drake, who shot you?"

"It was your boy, Pete."

"What, are you serious?"

"Did you tell him that it was over between us? He came over here talking about how he was going to take care of my baby like it was his own. When I heard that, I just went crazy, I started beating his ass and then, out of nowhere, he pulled a gun out and shoots me and ran off. He's going to be sorry that he ever laid eyes on me."

"Drake, please don't do anything that you will be sorry for."

"Oh, I won't be sorry for anything that I will do to him."

"I feel like this is all my fault. I told him we were over because I was mad at you, but I didn't know he was going to come over and tell you that bullshit about raising your baby."

Pete packed a bag, left his dad a note and headed out. He was going to stay with his cousin's in Columbus, Ohio. He didn't know if Drake was dead or alive. He didn't even know where he shot him, he just knew he shot him.

Pete pulled onto the interstate and headed for his cousin. He was afraid that the police will come looking for him so he was getting out of dodge.

He wanted to reach out to Adriane, but he didn't know if she had heard the news yet so he would wait for her call.

Adriane stood there looking at Drake.

"Are you coming home when they release me?" Drake asked.

"I don't know."

"You know I'm going to need a ride and I will need someone to help me out.

"I figured you would call your girl Megan for that."

"You're so funny."

"I'm not joking."

"Baby, are we going to let what we have come to an end because of your evil sister?"

"I had nothing to do with that, that's all your doing all by yourself. Not once I have invited her into our relationship, but you have several times. You keep inviting that sick bitch in and look what she's done. She has humiliated me and you over the internet."

"I know and I 'm sorry, but I know she drugged me."

"Drake I don't know if I can forgive so easily. It's going to take some time and if one more incident happens with Megan and you, then I'm done for good. I'll just be a single mom."

"I promise, nothing else will happen. You have my word."

"Yeah we will see."

"Why don't you hop your sexy ass in this bed with me."

"Boy, you're crazy."

"No, I'm serious."

"Oh my God, I forgot Renee's out in the lobby."

"Why did you bring her? I wanted you to stay the night with me."

"I can't spend the night here."

"Yeah, you can."

"Oh no, I can't. I'm going home. I will be back tomorrow when they release you."

"You promise."

"I promise, but that doesn't mean I will move back in with you."

"Aw baby come on, move back in. I need you there with me."

"We will see. I'm not making any promises, I said I will see."

"Well, that's better than you saying no."

Adriane remained with Drake a little longer before saying goodbye. She kissed him passionately before leaving.

"Hey call me when you know what time you will be released."

"I will baby. I love you."

"I love you too," Adriane said as she left the room.

Adriane made her way back to the waiting room. Renee saw her coming and met her in the hallway.

"How is he?"

"Oh, he's fine. They're keeping him here overnight for observation. I can pick him up tomorrow." Adriane said as she and Renee walked out of the hospital to the parking garage.

"Did he say who shot him?"

"Yes, that stupid ass Pete."

"What, are you kidding me?'

"This is kind of my fault. I was mad at Drake for staying out all night so I wanted to get back at him by having dinner with Pete. I had no idea Pete would confront Drake."

"Girl, you are playing with fire. Drake ain't no joke in case you didn't know."

"What do you mean?" Adriane asked as she pulled out of the parking garage.

"Ask your brother John about Drake. I don't know why you never saw Drake around the neighborhood, but he was always hanging around. He used to be part of the Ghetto boys crew."

"No!."

"Yes! He was something else. Everyone in the neighborhood was afraid of him."

"Dang, I don't remember ever seeing him. Where was your mind or should I say who was your mind on?"

"Drake is fine now, but back in the day, girl, he was super fine."

"Renee, can I ask you something and I need for you to be honest with me, did you ever sleep with Drake?"

"Girl, please I was never Drake's type. To be honest, Sharon wasn't even his type. She just continued to flirt with him and one day he decided to take her up on her offer and blew her fucking mind. That's all she talked about was Drake."

"But she never talked about him to me. I had no idea who Drake was."

"That's because she knew he liked you. He would always ask her about you and that would piss the hell out of her."

"Man, that's crazy that I never knew any of this and I didn't even know he existed."

"So how did you meet him then?"

"I met him the day of Connie's party. When I left I took a short cut through the woods and he was there."

"Now why would you do that?"

"I wanted to get home quick. You know I was pissed at Katie and Pete."

"That's too funny. I guess you liked what you saw."

"No doubt, that ass blew me away, but at first, I didn't actually see his face because he had a helmet on, but he intrigued me so
that I went back later that night and that's when I saw his gorgeous ass. It was too funny because he sneaked up behind

me. It was like he knew I was going to come back so he was waiting for me, well that's how it seemed."

"Man, I wish I could have been there. So is that why you and Sharon got into a fist fight?"

"Sure is. She got mad because I came over. They were inside when I heard him telling her that it was over and that's when I knocked on the door and she came out asking me why I was over there."

"I hate to tell you this, but Sharon and Megan used to be good friends some years back."

"And where was I? I never saw Megan until I started seeing Drake."

"Girl, I don't know where your mind was back then, but you were right there. You had to have seen Megan and Drake." Adriane pulled up in front of Renee's house. She cut the engine as the two continued to talk.

"I don't remember either one of them, but I wish I did. Are you sure I was around when Drake and Megan were around."

"I know you were. Remember when Raymond's dad threw that block party on 30th street and five people got shot?"

"Yeah, I remember. There was a gang of us that walked together."

"Drake and Megan were walking with us."

"That's too funny that I don't remember them. I wonder if I saw a picture of them from back in the day if I would remember them."

"Let me check my photo album to see if I have any pictures and if I do, I will bring them by tomorrow."

"You know Drake mentioned that he knew me and my brothers, but damn why can't I remember him."

"Maybe it wasn't meant for you to see him back then."

"That just might be true."

The next morning, Adriane got a phone call from Drake telling her that he had been released.

"Okay, babe I'm on my way."

Adriane arrived to find Drake patiently waiting for her arrival.

"It's about time you got here. I am so ready to go home."

"I'm sorry, but I had to make a couple of stops."

"Oh just leave me waiting. I see how important I am to you."

"Whatever, looks like someone is cranky this morning."

"Yes, I am. I'm feeling a little neglected right now."

"Who's neglecting you," Adriane asked as she bent over to kiss Drake on the lips.

"My soon to be wife and baby mama."

Adriane walked along side of him as the nurse pushed him through the doors.

"Now stay right here while I pull the car up."

"Where am I going to go?"

"You're going to go to hell in a handbasket if you don't be nice."

Adriane and the nurse laughed.

"I see you got jokes this morning."

Adriane pulled the car up, got out and helped Drake get into the passenger seat.

"Now let's make sure the baby is fastened up." Drake looked at Adriane. Adriane doesn't pay him any attention. She's busy trying not to laugh. She knew he was irritated with her for taking her time picking him up, but she stopped by the house and has something special planned for him when he gets home.

Denise Hill

CHAPTER NINETEEN

On the way home, Drake was beginning to irritate Adriane.

"Did you see your boy Pete?'

"No, why would I."

"You started this bullshit telling him we were through and kissing him in the parking lot."

"No, if I remember correctly, you started this. All of our problems have been because of your actions, so don't blame this bullshit as you say, on me. You had no business following me in the first fucking place. I only told Pete we were through because I knew he would not meet with me. I was angry with you and I wanted to get back at you and that's why I allowed Pete to kiss me and second you're the one who fucked and stayed overnight with that bitch Megan and don't get me started on Sharon. Right now, deep down inside, I am still pissed at you so don't start no shit with me because I will let your ass to fend for yourself."

Drake laughed.

"Damn, you're cold."

"Cold as an icebox."

"I'm so sorry babe. I never meant to hurt you at all. Believe it or not, you mean the world to me and I don't want to live without you. I've had my eyes on you from the very first time I saw you, but I waited because I knew once I had an opportunity with you, I would never let you go. So, I got all my playboys ways out of my system so I can devote all my time to you."

"Um, sounds good, but not sure if I really believe you right now."

"You don't have to. Actions speak a lot louder than words."

"You got that right," Adriane said as she looked over at Drake. "Like your actions the other night?"

"Naw, babe, you can't hold that against me. Megan had to have drugged me. There is no way I would have spent the night with her let alone have sex with her, you have to believe me on that. I would never do that to you."

"What happens when she comes back and says, Drake, I 'm pregnant because you know that's what she wants?"

"I'll have to deal with that if that happens, but I do know one thing, I will never leave you because of that, not matter what."

"Drake got both sisters pregnant, I can just hear it now. Do you know how that would make me feel? I would always have some kind of hatred in my heart for you for doing this. What I don't
understand is why you would even meet her somewhere. Does she have some type of hold on you?"

"Hell naw, I met with her because she said she had a gift for us."

"And you believed her. Why are you men so damn gullible when it comes to women? I just don't understand. It's just like Pete meeting with me. I really don't understand him meeting with me after you kicked his ass for trying to force himself on me."

"Please don't talk about him anymore. I'm going to deal with him later on this issue here."

"Drake, please just leave it alone. I'm not trying to go to your funeral."

"Trust me, you won't."

"And I'm not trying to make visits to you in prison either." Adriane pulled up to the house, cut the engine and got out. She walked around to the passenger side, opened the door and helped Drake out.
The two walked slowly to the house, Adriane inserted the key and unlocked the door. She allowed Drake to enter first and when he did, he got the surprise of his life. Not only was it his birthday, but it's their three month anniversary.

"Happy Birthday baby," Adriane said as she kissed him on the lips.

"You remembered."

"Of course I remembered. Is that why you were so cranky because you thought I forgot? Not only is it your birthday, but it's our three month anniversary. "Happy Anniversary!"
The house was decorated with balloons, gifts, and a huge birthday cake.

"You can't touch anything. I have invited some friends over and they should be arriving shortly to celebrate with us."

"Why so early?"

"Because I wanted this evening to be just for us. I want us to celebrate in our own special way."

Twenty minutes later, people started arriving, bringing gifts and food. Adriane had invited his staff, his friends, her friends and her family. Drake's sister was still out of the country so she couldn't invite her and his parents are no longer living. The party was going as planned. Drake was opening his birthday gifts and cards when he grabbed the last birthday card. He opened it and read the card out loud.

HAPPY BIRTHDAY, DRAKE, I HOPE THIS WILL BE A MEMORABLE DAY FOR YOU. I HOPE ALL YOUR WISHES COME TRUE.

P.S.
I LEFT A GIFT FOR YOU TO WATCH IN THE DVD PLAYER. ENJOY!!!!!

"Well, let's see what's in the DVD player." One of Drake's friends shouted!

Drake walked over to the TV, turned it on and then turned on the DVD player. He waited for both to turn on and then he pushed play.

Drake and the attendees were not prepared for what they were about to see.

When the video came on, it was Drake and Megan having sex.

"Oh shit!" Someone yelled out.

"Drake!" Adriane shouted. She was so embarrassed.

Drake quickly turned the TV off.

"How the hell did that get in here?" The room went silent. Adriane's parents looked in disbelief.

Then out of nowhere, Mr. Oliver walked up to Drake and Adriane.

"Don't let Satan steal your joy. This is a day of celebration so let's continue to celebrate.

The crowd cheered, but Adriane was annoyed. "Megan had to be dealt with." She thought to herself.

Two hours later, the house was quiet. The only people there were Drake, Adriane, and Renee. Drake was relaxing in the chair in the living room, while Adriane and Renee were cleaning up the kitchen and putting things away.

"How did that DVD get in here?" Renee whispered to Adriane.

"That stupid bitch was here while I was gone."

"She still has a key?"

"She gave Drake a key back, but she must have made a copy."

"I felt so sorry for you guys."

"What you guys need to do is to put up so video camera's so you can catch her on video and go to the police."

Adriane pulled Renee aside and whispered. "I didn't tell you, but I found out that Megan is my biological sister.

"Are you serious?"

"Yes, I wish I was just kidding. I hate to say I am related to someone like that."

"She's crazy just like her brother."

"You know about him?"

"Girl yes, everyone around here does."

"Damn, I feel so left out. How is it that everyone that I know, knows this family, but I had no clue about them?'

"I don't know what to tell you since you've lived in this area for ten years. Like I said before, maybe it wasn't meant for you to know them back then."

"You're probably right. I wish I didn't know them now."

"Really, I haven't heard you mention anything about your birth parents, have you met them yet?"

"Nope, I'm not ready for that just yet. I don't know if I will ever be ready. Renee, thanks for helping me clean up this mess."

"No problem. I'm actually enjoying our time together without Sharon."

"Oh, don't mention that name to me."

"Here, let me walk you out."

Adriane and Renee walked to the front door.

"Goodbye, Drake I hoped you enjoyed your birthday."

"Thanks, Renee, I had a great time."

Adriane walked over to Drake, bent down and gave him a kiss.

"How are you feeling?"

"Sleepy, the pain medicine just started to kick in and it's making me sleepy."

"Why don't we go and lay down and take a nap so you will be ready for tonight."

"What's happening tonight?"

"Well, I wanted us to go out to dinner, dancing, and maybe a little you know what."

"Baby I would love to do that, but right now, I'm just not feeling up to it."

"I understand babe. You just got shot yesterday and here I am planning a full evening of events, how selfish of me. We have plenty of time to do those things." Adriane said as she and Drake walked down the hall to their bedroom.

As soon as Drake hit the bed, he was out like a light. It didn't take Adriane long to fall asleep either.

Megan parked down the street from Drake's house. She pulled a flashlight out of the glove compartment and pulled some plastic gloves from her pocket before getting out of the car. Megan looked around to see if anyone was out before she headed through the woods to Drake's house.

As Megan approached the house, she saw Drake's and Adriane's car parked in the driveway. She walked over to Adriane's car and let the air out of the tires. She walked over to Drake's car, pulled a knife out of her boots and stabbed each tire. She then walked around to the back of the house, and with the flashlight, she broke the basement window and crawled through. As she crawled through, she cut her arm on the broken glass in the window.

"Dammit," She said as she looked around for something to wipc the blood off her arm.

Adriane awoke when she heard the sound of glass breaking. She nudged Drake.

"Drake, I think someone has broken a window."

"What?" Drake said as he stirred awake.

Adriane got up out of the bed and walked toward the door.

"No, stay here," Drake said as he got up. "I'll go and check it out."

Drake walked out the room and down the hall to the kitchen. He looked around the room when he heard a noise coming from the basement.

He went back to the bedroom, pulled open the drawer and got his gun out.

"Oh my God Drake, please be careful."

"Just stay here."

Megan heard movement upstairs and froze in her tracks. She stood still and listened as the footsteps get closer and closer. She heard the basement door knob turn and seconds later, the door opened. Megan panicked and ran to the window, crawled out cutting herself again and ran through the woods. Megan was running when she turned to look back as she heard someone following behind her and hit her head on a thick branch and fell to the ground. Megan was knocked out for a minute or so and when she came too, someone was standing over her looking down at her. And all at once, the person disappeared. Megan slowly got up, looked around and shook her head. Megan thought it was just her imagination.

Denise Hill

CHAPTER TWENTY

Drake made his way down to the basement. It was pitch black so he held onto the railing as he took one step at a time. Once he came to the last step, he felt along the wall for the light switch. Once he found the light switch, he flicked it on and moved further into the room. He looked to his left and he sees the broken window and the blood.

Drake walked over to the window and peered out. The coast was clear so he searched the basement for any sign of an intruder.

Meanwhile, Adriane got tired of waiting for Drake to return, so she took it upon herself to go and find him. Adriane opened the door slowly and listened before stepping out into the hallway. She didn't hear anything so she continued down the hall to the living room. She didn't see Drake so she moved to the kitchen where she saw the door to the basement opened. Adriane walked over, stood at the top of the stairs of the basement and listened for any movement. She heard movement and called out to Drake.

"Drake, are you down here?"

"Yes, it's me."

"Is it okay if I come down?"

"Yeah, just watch your step."

Adriane walked down the steps and when she reached the bottom step, she saw Drake trying to put plastic up to the window.

"What happened?"

Drake didn't really want to tell Adriane what had happened because he didn't want her to freak out.

"Drake?"

"Someone broke the window."

"Oh my God!"

"Drake you need to call the police and then put up some security cameras so we can catch whoever is coming around here."

"Yeah, you're right, because right now, I don't feel good leaving you here by yourself."

"Do you think it could have been Megan?"

"I don't know. I wouldn't put anything past her."

"Well, once we catch that ass on video, we can prosecute her."

"Can you hand me that tape over there and hold this up while I tape this plastic up to the window."

"Sure."

"Wait, I think I have some more tape in my truck. It will probably work better."

Drake ran upstairs and out the door to his truck. He went inside his glove compartment and pulled out some heavy duty tape. He was on his way back inside when he looked over at Adriane's car and sees her tire are flat. The closer he got, he sees all four tires are flat. He looked over at his truck and his tires are flat as well.

"Damn, I know Megan did this." He said out loud. Drake walked back inside, down the hall to his room and grabbed his phone. He called the police.

Megan ran inside the house and ran straight to the bathroom. Her cut was deeper than she thought and was bleeding bad.

"Megan, what happened?" Her mom asked.

"I cut myself on some glass."

"Let me see. Megan, this looks bad. You should go to the ER."

"You think so?"

"Yes, do you want me to take you?'

"Yes, if you don't mind."

Megan grabbed a towel and wrapped it around her arm and headed out the door with her mom.

While waiting for Megan at the emergency room. Mrs. Brown decided to call Drake to check on Adriane.

"Hello, Drake how are you?"

"I'm good, Mrs. Brown. I have a little situation over here right now."

"What's going on with you?"

"I'm here at the ER with Megan so I decided to call and check on Adriane. How is she doing?"

"What happened to Megan?"

Drakes wanted confirmation that Megan cut her arm so he will have her red handed.

"Megan cut her arm on some glass or something. She's getting stitches right now."

"Oh really. Well, you know she came over her and broke my basement window, that is how she probably cut her arm and she also cut my tires and let the air out of Adriane's tires. I just called the police so they will be visiting Megan soon."

"Aw Drake, why would you do that?"

"Why would I do what? Why would your daughter continue to bother me and Adriane? That's what you should be asking Megan instead of trying to take up for her. Mrs. Brown, I have to go."

Drake said as he disconnected the call. He was a little irritated with Mrs. Brown right now.

Drake made his way back down to the basement and decided to leave the plastic down until the police arrive.

"I just found out that Megan is in the ER getting stitches."

"What are you serious?"

"Yes, Mrs. Brown just called to check on you and told me she was at the ER with Megan and that she cut her arm on some glass. Oh, and when I went outside to get this tape." Drake held up the tape. "I noticed our tires were flat. I just called the police and I told Mrs. Brown what Megan had done and that the police would be over to see Megan, she asked me why would I do that. Man, your family is off the chain."

"See, this is why I have no desire to meet them. Sometimes you just have to leave things alone."

"I know, but she's still your mother and our baby's grandmother. Are you going to take that away from her?"
"I haven't even thought about it."

Minutes later, the police arrived. They took samples of the blood left behind on the broken glass, took pictures of the window and the tires. They wrote down Megan's information and told Drake that they would be in touch.
Drake and Adriane stood on the porch talking to the police.
"I will bet money, Megan is the one that hit me in my head."
"I had my doubts at first, but now, I wouldn't put anything past her."
"I told him that we need to get some security camera so we can catch whoever it is."
"Yeah, that sounds like a good idea." One of the police officers said.

Megan had been in the ER for three hours before they finished stitching her. She walked out to find her mother asleep in the chair.
Megan nudged her mother.
"Mom we can leave."
"Well, it's about time."
"I know, tell me about it."
Once they got in the car, Mrs. Brown asked Megan if she had been over to Drake's and if she had broken his window and flattens their tires.
"Mom, you know I wouldn't do that."
"He said he's sending the police to our house. You know how I feel about that. I will never forget how the neighbors looked at us when they came and got Michael."
"I know mom, don't worry. I didn't do anything and they can't prove that I did."
"So did you call Drake or did he call you?"

"I called him to check on Adriane."

"Why, why do you even care about her? It's obvious she doesn't care about you and dad. If she cared she would have met with you guys already. Adriane is so selfish mom."

"Megan, that's your sister. You guys need to get to know each other."

"Yeah, right. Mom, do you honestly think I am going to befriend her. She's with Drake and she's having his baby. Mom, I still love Drake."

"You mean to tell me I'm going to be a grandma. Oh my God, I can't wait."

Megan looked over at her mom and rolled her eyes.

"Do you think she's really going to let you be a part of that baby's life? I wouldn't hold my breath."

"I believe she will. I just have to give her some time."

"Okay."

After the police had left, Drake called some of his buddies and they took him to get some new tires for his cars.
He didn't want to leave Adriane alone at the house, but she insisted that she would be just fine.
By the time the guys finished changing the tires, it was pitch dark. The guys lingered around a little while longer sitting on the porch drinking beer and talking.

"Hey, I didn't want to say anything to you in front of Adriane, but what's up with the video?" One of his friends asked.

"Man, that bitch Megan is trying her best to break me and Adriane up. She drugged me, man. I don't remember any of that."

"Man, I wish some sexy chic would drug and take advantage of me like that," His other friend said.

"You're silly as hell," Drake said as he laughed at his buddy.

Adriane was inside cooking dinner and remembered the window downstairs.

"Oh shit." She said as she walked out onto the porch.

"Hey Drake, don't forget to put plastic up to the basement window."

"Man, I'm glad you reminded me. Can you guys help me with the basement window?"

The men walked into the kitchen to get to the basement.

"Adriane you got it smelling good in here.

"Thanks. I have enough in case you guys would like to join us for a late dinner."

They all looked at Drake.

"Sure, it's fine."

After the men finished with the window, they washed their hands and sat down to dinner. Adriane had fried some perch and catfish, with fries, coleslaw, hushpuppies and made some country time lemonade.

The men wasted no time in piling their plate with food. The table was quiet the only sounds you heard were forks hitting the plate and men smacking their lips.

"I'm going to start coming around here more often if I can get cooked meals like this."

ENVY

CHAPTER TWENTY-ONE

Drake and Adriane were sleeping when Drake awoke to the sound of something hitting the floor. He looked around the room and then he looked over at Adriane, who was knocked out. Drake eased out of bed and made his way out into the hall. He stood there to see if he heard any movement before heading to the living room. When he didn't, he walked slowly and quietly down the hall to the living room.

When Drake made it to the living room, he turned on the living room light and when he did, he sees a shadow run past the window. Drake ran to the front door, opened it and stepped out onto the porch. Drake stood with his back up against the screen door listening. He continued to stand there and was still standing there when Adriane walked up behind him on the inside of the house and knocked on the door causing Drake to jump. Adriane laughed.

"What are you doing?" She asked as she tried to open the door, but Drake's weight was preventing her from opening the door.

Drake turned to her with his finger up to his mouth trying to keep her quiet

Drake made his way over to the side of the porch and looked out, but because the porch light was off he was unable to see. Drake turned around and decided to go back inside when he stepped on some glass.

"Ouch, he yelled. Drake hopped inside the house where he sees a piece of glass sticking out of his foot. "Where did this come from?" He asked.

Adriane helped him to the couch and pulled the glass from his foot.

"Why wasn't the porch light on? It was on before we went to bed."

"I don't know," Adriane said as she walked over to the light switch.

"Well the light switch is on, maybe the bulb blew out. Let me get another one. Drake, you need to make sure you get all the glass out and put some pressure on your foot to help stop the bleeding." Adriane said as she walked passed Drake headed to the kitchen to get another light bulb.

When Adriane walked outside with the bulb and flashlight in hand, she sees that the bulb had been broken and the glass that Drake stepped on was the bulb. Adriane moved back inside quickly.

"Drake, I think someone broke the bulb. The glass is what you stepped on."

"But who would do that?" Drake asked.

"The same person who broke the basement window."

"Naw, I don't think it was Megan."

"How do you know?"

"I don't, but my gut is telling me different. What if it was Pete?"

"I forgot about him. We need to install a security camera and more lights as soon as possible." Adriane said.

"I agree."

"I will go to Lowes in the morning and get some more lights and check into getting a security camera," Drake said as sat putting pressure on his foot.

"I have to say it is getting a little weird around here," Adriane said.

"I know. It seems so surreal. I hope you're not having second thoughts about moving in here with me."

Adriane looked at Drake as she tried to find the right words to say. "I don't regret anything, I just want to be safe. I want us to be safe."

"I understand totally. I would hate for something bad to happen to you or the baby. Right now, let's just see how this week goes. It might be a good idea for you to move back home with your parents until things die down."

Adriane nodded her head. "Do you really think it's someone other than Megan?"

"I do."

"Okay, I think it's time for me to sit down and meet my biological family. I want them to know what's going on just in case it's not Megan, but if we find out that it's, Megan, I want her to go to jail or get the help that she needs."

"Okay, we can do that. I will make the call in the morning."

The next day as Drake promised, he phoned the Brown's and set a time for him and Adriane to come over and talk to them about what they suspected.

Adriane was feeling a little nervous meeting her biological parents for the first time. She remembered when she was young how she couldn't wait for this day, but now, she doesn't feel the same way and now she wished, she would have stayed home.

Drake pulled into the Brown's driveway, cut the engine and got out. He headed around the car to the passenger side where Adriane sat looking up at the house.

Drake opened her door. "Are you okay?"

"No, not really. Is it too late for me to change my mind?"

"Yes," Drake said as he helped her out of the car. "Let's just go and get this over with once and for all. I guarantee you will feel much better once you do so."

"I hope you're right," Adriane said as she held onto Drake as they made their way up the walkway.

Before they got to the front porch, the door opened and there stood Megan with a bandage around her arm.

Adriane looked at Drake. "See I told you it was that bitch."

"Who you calling a bitch, you hoe."

"I must be a good one and that's why I have Drake and you don't?"

Megan ran up to Adriane, but Drake stepped in front of her. "Oh, no you don't," Drake said as he held onto Megan. "Not today sweetheart."

By this time, Mr. & Mrs. Brown rushed to the door. "Oh my God! Mrs. Brown cried out as her husband held on to her with tears in his eyes.

Adriane stood there, the feeling that went through her surprised her and tears started to form in her eyes.

Mrs. Brown walked up to Adriane and the two embrace each other. Mr. Brown walked over and placed his arms around both ladies.

"Our life is complete now." He said.

Megan stood there in disgust. "Oh, this is so sickening." She said as she walked back into the house.

Mrs. Brown looped her arm around Adriane's as they made their way inside. Drake and Mr. Brown follow behind them.

"They act like we are not even here." Mr. Brown said as he laughed.

"You noticed that too," Drake said.

The Browns, Drake, and Adriane sat and talked for hours. Mrs. Brown showed Adriane pictures of her other siblings and filled her in on what everyone was doing. She tried to stay away from asking her about the nurse who stole her, but she couldn't.

"Adriane, how was your childhood?"

"It was good once I moved in with the Oliver's. They were so nice to me and made me feel warm and welcomed. I felt like I finally belonged, but my parents that took me, now that's another story. I was verbally and sexually abused until they burned in the fire."

"Fire?" Mrs. Brown asked.

"Yes, our house caught on fire in the middle of the night and I was the only one that escaped."

Mrs. Brown grabbed a hold of Adriane's hand. "You poor baby."

"I know. I couldn't understand how someone would take me from my biological parents and raise me in a home full of abuse."

Mr. Brown just shook his head. "I guess in the end, they got what they deserved."

"Pretty much," Adriane said.

"Oh, did Megan tell you guys that I was pregnant?"

"Yes, she did. That's awesome. When's your due date?" Mrs. Brown asked.

"April 15th. I have a long way to go."

"It will be here before you know it." Mr. Brown said. "Are you guys getting married?'

"Yes, we are. Just as soon as the little gets here." Drake said.

"I know you and Megan are on bad terms right now Adriane, but I hope one day you guys can act like sisters instead of enemies."

"Um… she has done some awful things. It will take a miracle for that to happen.

"I have faith that God will work it out." Mrs. Brown said as she smiled at Adriane.

In the meantime, Megan sat out front in her car mad as hell. "This has got to be a nightmare." She said to herself. "How cruel can life be to someone. She has my man and is carrying his baby and now she's the apple of my parents' eyes. This is some fucking bullshit." Megan said as she got out of the car and walked up the walkway to the house. When she entered, she made her way to the family room where everyone was at. "Well, isn't this nice. It's like one big happy family, NOT." She said as she stood in the entryway of the family room.

"Megan, you know I didn't raise you to act like this." Mr. Brown said as he gave her the evil eye.

"And you didn't raise her at all, but now you're acting like dear old dad."

"Megan, if I didn't know any better, I would say you're jealous."

"Jealous! Jealous of what?"

Adriane laughed as she rubbed her belly trying to rub it in Megan's face that she's carrying Drake's baby and not her.

"I hope that baby comes out a retard," Megan said as she made her way down the hall to her bedroom.

"Megan, now you get back in here and apologize to Drake and your sister."

"That's okay, she doesn't have to. You know what they say, some people can and those who can't say harsh things."

"You can go somewhere with that lame ass shit," Megan yelled from down the hall.

Adriane could not believe how Megan was talking in front of their parents.

"You allow her to talk like this in front of you?"

"Megan is going through some things right now, so I try and pay her no attention." Mrs. Brown said.

"Yeah, but that's still no reason for her to walk around her disrespecting us either." Mr. Brown said.

Over the next couple weeks, Adriane started visiting her parents on a regular basis, but she and Megan were still at odds with each other. She hated the sight of Megan and Megan hated her even more. Megan thought of ways to torment Adriane so she would leave Drake, but every time she tried, it would always backfired in her face.

The bigger Adriane's stomach got, the more Megan hated her. Megan would lay awake in bed crying her eyes out over Drake. She couldn't understand why she couldn't get pregnant with his baby. Megan prayed every night that something bad would happen to Adriane's baby, but the more she prayed, the more Adriane seemed to blossom in everyone's eyes, especially Drake's.

Denise Hill

CHAPTER TWENTY-TWO

It was Halloween and Adriane had decorated the house in hopes of some trick or treaters, but being that their home has had such a negative impact on the community, she hoped to change that this year. She had posted fliers in town and in the neighborhood about her and Drake and how they would be handing out candy.

Drake and Adriane had been sitting on the front porch for about an hour and not one trick or treater.

"Well, at least I tried babe."

"Yes, you did sweetheart."

Just then, a group of teenagers appeared at the entrance of the house.

"Come on up," Adriane yelled as she and Drake stood up and watched the teenagers slowly make their way to the porch.

"Are you guys afraid?"

"I'm not afraid." The littlest one said as he reached for the bag of candy that Adriane had in her hand. The others followed suit. Adriane and Drake could tell that they had loosened up as Adriane continued to talk with them. They stood there for about fifteen minutes talking with Drake and Adriane and then another group arrived with their parents. It warmed Drake's heart to see how loving and caring Adriane was with the kids. He just knew she would make a great mom.

Later that night, Adriane and Drake retired to the living room as they sat hugged up together watching TV.

"I can't believe how many trick or treaters we had," Adriane said.

"I know." Drake was in mid-sentence when a brick comes flying through the living room window just missing his head and the side of Adriane's face.

"Oh my God!" Adriane screamed.

Drake jumped up, he made sure Adriane was okay before running to the front door and running outside. He thought he saw a shadow of someone running to the back of the house. Drake took off after this person, but because he hadn't installed the lights like Adriane asked him, he was unable to see anything.

Drake stood in the backyard in the dark listening for any sounds of movement.

Adriane stood in the doorway with a bat in hand. She made her way off the porch and moved to the side of the house when she sees a shadow approaching. She raised the bat, but Drake appeared out of the darkness.

"Babe, what are you doing out here?"

"I wanted to be out here just in case you needed some help." Drake laughed as he took the bat out of her hand. "You are one tough cookie I see."

"I will fight for what's mine."

"Oh really?"

"Yes, I thought you knew that by now."

"I do now."

Come on, let's get back inside.

Drake and Adriane begin to clean up the glass and when they were almost finished, Drake said.

"Why don't you finish cleaning this up while I go down to the basement to get some board so I can board up this window. After everything was completed, they stood there trying to figure out who had done this. I say it was that damn Megan." Adriane said.

"I think not. I believe it was Pete."

"Is there any way to get fingerprints off a brick?" Adriane asked.

Drake chuckled.

"What's funny?"

"You are," Drake said as he moved closer to Adriane. He pulled her hair away from her face and moved closer as he brushed his lips up against hers.

"Oh, my God! I love the way you smell. It turns me on every time you wear that perfume. You know what I believe you wear it on purpose because you know what it does to me."

"Boy, Boo! I wear it because I like the way it smells." Adriane said as she took a step back.

"Boy! Where you see a boy at? You know this is all man right here." Drake said he grabbed his manhood.
Adriane rolled her eyes at Drake and shook her head. "So this is what makes you a man and not a boy?" Adriane said as she moved his hand and replaced it with her hand.

"I'm going to let you answer that one for yourself," Drake said as he caressed one of Adriane's breasts.

"Um… Are you trying to turn me on, Drake?"

"Um… Now, why would I do that Adriane?"
They both laughed as Adriane put her arms around Drake's neck. "I love you so much, Drake. I have no idea what I would do if you ever decided to leave me."

"As long as you are faithful to me, you will never have to worry about that until God calls me home."

"You promise?" Adriane asked as she looked up at Drake.

"I promise baby," Drake said as he bent down to kiss her on the tip of her nose. "Now come on back here with me so I can show you just how much I love you."

"Let's go," Adriane said as she followed behind Drake.

Thirty minutes later, they were fast asleep.
The next morning, Drake made his way to Lowe's again to talk to someone about coming out and replacing the living room window.

"I see you're back again." The young female clerk said.

"Yeah, someone threw a brick through our window last night."

"Now who would want to do something like that to such a handsome man as yourself."

"You never know," Drake said, ignoring her last statement.

"How soon can I get someone to come out and replace my living room window. Drake asked the male clerk.

"Let me check out the schedule. Do you have something up to the window now?"

"Yes, I have a board up to it right now."

The clerk continued to look at the schedule book when the female clerk stepped from around the counter and stood right next to Drake.

"Damn you smell good." She said.

"He sure does," Adriane said as she walked up.

"Bitch back up," Adriane said as she eyed the clerk.

The clerk had no idea Drake was with anyone and by the looked Adriane was giving her, she knew not to start any mess with her.

"Oh, I 'm sorry. I meant no disrespect.

"Wasn't none taken," Adriane said.

Drake tried his best not to laugh, but the way Adriane showed up was just too funny. He had no idea she was even in the store. She told him that she didn't feel like getting out.

Drake looked over at Adriane who's busy eyeing the clerk. He took his hand and turned her face until she's facing him.

"You are one special lady, you know that, don't you?"

"You better make sure these little skanks know that."

"I only have eyes for you sweetheart."

"Sir, I can have someone come out tomorrow around noon. Will that work?"

"Yes, noon will be fine."

As Drake and Adriane left the store, Sharon stood in the entrance as she watched Drake and Adriane drive away. Her heart ached every day for Drake. She loved Drake from the first time she laid eyes on him as a young girl, but it wasn't until she was older and he and Megan had broken up that he

even noticed and gave her the time of day and now to think he's with Adriane, she just couldn't take it.
She just found out that Adriane was pregnant, which infuriated her even more.

As Drake and Adriane pulled out of the Lowe's parking lot, Adriane's stomach growled.

"Oh my God! Was that your stomach?" Drake asked.
Adriane laughed.

"Yes. I guess I need to eat.'

"What do you have a taste for?"

"I don't know. I guess at this point, anything will do."

"Right and as soon as I pull up somewhere you will be saying oh I don't want to eat here."

"Stop it. Just pull into IHOP. There are a variety of things for me to choose from."
As Drake and Adriane walk into IHOP, Drake's phone rang. It was coming from a private number. He started to let it go to voicemail, but decided to answer it.

"Hello."

"I see your bitch is pregnant. Let's just see if she lives long enough to give birth to it."

"Who is this?" Drake asked as he looked around.

"Aw, don't worry about who I am, just worry about keeping your bitch safe until she gives birth to that bastard, but if you can't shame on you, Drake." The clock is ticking tick tock tick tock." Then the phone goes dead.
The phone call bothered Drake, but not for his sake, but for Adriane's and his unborn child.
Adriane sees the horror on Drake's face.

"Babe, what's wrong? Who was that on the phone?"

"Nobody, it was the wrong number."

"Are you sure? You look like you just seen a ghost."

"Naw, I'm good," Drake said as he grabbed a hold of Adriane's hand and followed the waitress to their booth.

All through brunch, Adriane had to keep touching Drake under the table with her foot. His mind seemed to be somewhere else, which made Adriane think something was up with the phone call he received.

"You think I should get an abortion?" Adriane asked Drake just to see if he's paying any attention.

"Babe, that's up to you?"

"Oh, so you don't want this baby now?"

"What, what are you talking about?" Drake finally tuned in to hear the last part of the conversation.

"I wanted to see if you were paying attention to me and just like I thought your mind was somewhere else. I asked if you wanted me to get an abortion and you said it was up to me."

"I'm sorry babe, but you better not get rid of my seed."

"I'm not I was just playing and besides, it's too late for that."

ENVY

CHAPTER TWENTY-THREE

Drake was still shooken up about the phone call he received earlier. He vowed to do everything in his power to keep Adriane and the baby safe, but how could he when he had no clue as to who would want to harm them. It could be anyone and how can he protect them at all times.

Drake walked out onto the porch and pulled out his cell phone and called John, Adriane's brother.

"Hey John, this is Drake how are you?"

"I'm good bro and you?"

"I'm not so good right now. I need to talk to you face to face. Can you stop by when you have a chance?"

"Sure, I can stop by right after work. Is Adriane okay?"

"Yeah, she's fine."

"Okay, well, I will see you guys this evening."

"Alright, thanks, John."

Drake continued to stand outside on the porch. His mind was going a mile a minute. He was debating on telling Adriane about the call. He wanted to tell her, but he didn't want her to worry.

After debating with himself, Drake decided to tell Adriane when John arrived, but in the meantime, he had to go into the office for a bit, but he refused to leave Adriane alone.

Drake walked into the house and down the hall to their bedroom. He stood at the door and watched as Adriane slept soundly. He moved further into the room until he reached the bed and bent down to take a seat. He could hear Adriane breathing slightly.

"Adriane," Drake called out to her as he shook her softly.
Adriane turned over. "What's wrong?"

"I need to go into the office and I want you to go with me. I don't want to leave you alone."

"And why not? You have before. Does this have anything to do with that phone call earlier?"

Drake sat there for a minute before answering.

"Yes, it does."

"So I guess it must have been the same phone call I received while sitting in the car at Lowes."

Drake looked over at her. "What call?"

"While l I was sitting out in the car I received a call from someone threatening me and the baby. They said if luck was on my

side, I would live to see my baby and if not, I deserved everything I was going to get."

Drake stood and began to pace back and forth.

"Could you tell who it was or if it was a male or female?"

"No, I couldn't tell."

"That's it, you're coming with me to the office and later this evening John is going to stop by. We are going to get to the bottom of this."

"Drake, it's only Megan and I wouldn't put too much into her threats."

"And what if it's not Megan, then what?"

"Then it's probably Pete."

"And you know what he did to me," Drake said as he pointed to his wound.

"I really don't believe Pete would really hurt me, you maybe, but not me."

"Well, I am not putting anything past anyone now let's go sleepy head."

Adriane got up from the bed and stood in front of Drake.

"You're so cute when you try to take charge."

"For your information young lady, I'm not trying to do anything, I'm doing the damn thing," Drake said as he bent down and kissed Adriane. "And I love it Popi," Adriane said as she wrapped her arms around Drake's waist and pulled him closer to her.

"I want some of this." She said grabbing his crotch.

"Is that so."

"Yes, I want it now."

"Too bad you're going to have to wait until we return. I have something important to do at the office so stop trying to tempt me and get dressed." Drake said as he backed out of the bedroom with his eyes on Adriane.

In the office, Drake sat behind his desk as he talked on the phone to his client while Adriane made herself comfortable as she stretched out on the couch.

Adriane dozed off and an hour later, she awoke to the sound of Drake and a female arguing outside the office in the hall.

Adriane got up off the couch and moved closer to the door when she recognized Megan's voice.

"Oh, this bitch is crazy," Adriane said as she snatched open the door.

"What is it going to take for you to see that he doesn't want your stupid ass?"

Megan turned to face Adriane. "He only wants you because of that bastard you're carrying."

"At least I can carry one."

Megan lunged at Adriane, but Drake blocked her path.

"Are you stupid? Do you think I'm going to allow you to hit my fiancée?"

"Drake you better get this bitch out of here before I beat her ass."

"I wish you would try," Megan said.

"Your wish is my command bitch," Adriane said as she stepped from around Drake and threw a punch that hit Megan in the eye.

Drake grabbed Megan and pushed her back.

"That's it, you have got to go," Drake said as he pulled Megan down the hall while Adriane stood there with her hands on her hips smiling.

"Bye, see you later," Adriane said.

Minutes later, Drake walked back to the office.

"What the hell is your problem?" He said as he looked at Adriane.

"What, what are you talking about? I'm here because you wanted me to be here. It's not my fault you can't keep your bitches in check." Adriane said as she rolled her eyes.

"I'm pissed because you're pregnant, Adriane."

"Is it true you are only with me because of the baby?"

"Oh my God! Now I know you do not believe that crap Megan said. I am with you because I love you and if you were not pregnant, I would still be with you and you know it."

"Why was Megan here?"

"The same reason as always."

Adriane walked closer to Drake. Tell me something, does my sister suck your dick as good as I do?" Adriane said as she unbuckled Drake's belt.

"Adriane, don't ask me no bullshit like that."

Adriane unfastened Drake's pants and pulled his dick out. She dropped down to her knees and grabbed a hold of the base of his penis as she ran her tongue across the tip.

"Well, does she?" Adriane asked as she inserted him into her mouth and deep throated him.

"Damn baby," Drake said as he placed his hand on the back of her head moving it back and forth.

"No baby, No. No one does it as good as you. Aw, shit Adriane." Drake screamed as the feeling curled his toes.

Just then, Adriane pulled away, walked over to the couch and removed her panties. She sat down and cocked her legs open, giving Drake a view of her treasure.

Adriane took her fingers and inserted two inside her as her thumb massaged her clit. Drake looked in awe.

Drake started stroking his penis as she slowly made his way over to Adriane.

"Damn baby, you sure know how to turn a nigga on."

Drake dropped to his knees removed Adriane's fingers and replaced it with his thick wet tongue. He slid his tongue slowly up and down her as he watched her shudder from his touch.

"Aw Drake please don't make me come just yet. I want to come with you inside me."

Drake continued to torture her with pleasure before inserting himself inside her tight wet juicy pussy.

"I see baby girl is wet just like I like it."

"Yes, she is. She will always be wet for you."

Drake began to move slowly in and out. He raised both legs in the air and goes even deeper.

"Oh my God Drake!" Adriane screamed.

"Come with me baby," Drake said.

"I'm coming, I'm coming. Adriane said.

Later that evening, John pulled up, cut the engine and exited the car.

He walked up the stairs to the house when Adriane ran out to greet him.

"Hey, John what's up?"

"Hey, baby girl how are you?"

John stood back to get a good look at Adriane. "Damn your stomach is getting out there."

"I know."

"How are you feeling these days?"

"You know I have my good days and then my bad days, but my good days outweigh my bad days so I can't complain."

"That's good. Where's that man of yours?"

"He's inside. Come on in. I made dinner in case you're hungry."

"You know I am always hungry."

John walked inside and was greeted by Drake.

"What's up Drake?' John asked.

"Man you don't even want to know."

"You guys have a seat while I fix your plates."

183

Drake and John take a seat at the kitchen table.

"Man, I don't even know where to start," Drake said.

"Well, you know Pete shot me over Adriane right."

"Yes, I know he did that."

"Then someone hit her in the head. Someone broke into the basement, and they broke our living room window yesterday and we both received threatening phone calls today. I think someone wants to harm Adriane. They don't want this baby to be born. She received a call this morning and so did I. The person said if she can make it to give birth, then they would let us be."

"So they want to play a fucking game to see if we can protect her until she gives birth."

"Pretty much."

"We need to get the police involved. Have you guys reached out to them?"

"No, I wanted to speak with you before doing so. You know if it was me, I wouldn't get the police involved I would handle things myself, but I fear for Adriane because I cannot always be around."

"I'm calling the cops now. I want them to know what's going on just in case I have to fuck someone up." John said as he pulled out his phone.

Denise Hill

CHAPTER TWENTY - FOUR

The police arrived in no time. Two officers walked around to the side of the house, while the one officer talked with Drake, Adriane and John inside as he questioned them about the incidents. The two officers around back looked for any evidence that could lead them to a suspect or suspects.

"Have either of you had any run- ins with anyone?" The first officer asked.

"No, not that would result in someone wanting to see Adriane and the baby dead," Drake answered.

"I just found out who my biological parents and siblings are, but before I knew that, my sister and I were at odds with each other and still are because she used to date Drake and she still wants him. We had a run in today at his office."

"Do you think she's behind this?" The officer asked.

"I do, but he doesn't," Adriane said.

"And why is that?" The officer asked.

"I just don't believe she's capable of actually harming someone."

"Well, keep in mind our brother is in prison now for murder," Adriane told Drake.

"Are you protecting her?" The police officer asked.

"Of course not, why would I?"

"I don't know. You tell me?" The officer said.

"So you think I'm protecting someone who could possibly hurt my unborn child and fiancee? What would I gain from doing that and if I thought it was her and I was protecting her, why would you even be here? I would definitely keep the police out of it if that was the case."

"I guess you have a point," John said.

"The only person I am trying to protect is Adriane and my child and I cannot do that all the time, that is why you're here," Drake said as he looked at the police officer and then turned to look at John.

"I believe you," John said as he threw his hands up.

"Can you write down the hours you work. We will try and have a police car outside your home or at least drive by several times during the day while you're at work." The police officer said.

Drake sat down and jotted down his work schedule and handed it to the officer.

"When will this window be fixed." The officer asked as he pointed to the living room window.

"They're coming out tomorrow," Adriane said.

"Here's my card. I want you to keep this with you at all times and if something doesn't seem right, be sure to give me a call. The officer said.

"I will. Thank you."

"Hey, I'm getting ready to head out and if you need anything, don't hesitate to call me. I'm not going to tell mom and dad about this because I don't want them to worry, but I know some people and I will have them look out for you as well."

"Okay, Thanks, John," Drake said.

"Hey sis, don't worry, I won't let anyone harm you."

"You know I'm not worried about myself. I just want my child to live."

"I know sis. I got you covered." John said as he hugged Adriane.

After everyone had left, Drake walked over and pulled Adriane to him.

"I hope you don't believe I am protecting Megan."

"No, if I really thought that, I wouldn't be here right now."

"I love you, but I'm not stupid."

"You're right about that."

The next day when the guy from Lowes arrived at Drake's, he found a dead squirrel tied to the front door.

He pulled out his phone and dialed Drake's number.

"Hello, this is David from Lowes and I'm out on your front porch and there's a dead squirrel tied to the front door. Drake walked over to the front door, opened it and unlocked the screen door. He sees the squirrel tied to the door handle of the screen.

"Wait just a minute." Drake went into the kitchen and looked through some drawers for an old rag. He then looked under the sink for a trash bag and walked back to the door. He untied the squirrel and grabbed it with the rag and shoved it into the trash bag.

"Do you need to come inside or are you going to work on the outside?"

"I can work on the outside first."

"Okay, just knock if you need anything." Drake walked back into the kitchen and found something to clean the door knob off with.

An hour later, the window was in and the guy was on his way back to Lowes.

"Hey babe, I'm going to head into the office. You are welcome to come with me if you like."

"Naw, I'm good. I will call you if things seem a little out of the ordinary." Adriane said as she stood on her tip toes to kiss Drake on the lips.

"Alright, but make sure you keep your phone with you at all times."

"I will and don't work too hard. Hey, what time will you be home?"

"I'm only working a few hours this week in the office so I should be home by three," Drake said as he looked down at his watch.

Adriane watched as Drake pulled off. She locked the screen and shut the front doors, as her phone rang.

"What are you doing home alone bitch?"

"Who is this?"

"Don't worry about who I am. You need to be worried about what I'm going to do to you when the time is right. I know you have the police car sitting at the entrance of your home. Don't think you can hide anything from me because I know your every move bitch. You're nasty bitch too. I saw you giving Drake some head in his office yesterday. A hoe like you must be good at giving head."

"You go to hell. You're nothing more than a coward. You can't even show your fucking face because you know I will kick your ass."

The caller laughed.

"Oh, really? Keep talking bad if you want because, in due time, I will see how bad you really are and just know you won't have Drake or John to rescue you."

"I don't need Drake or John to rescue me from the likes of you. You harass and threaten pregnant women. That says a lot about you, you fucking cunt. You know what, I have better things to do than to sit on this phone and argue with a coward like you. Bye bitch!" Adriane said as she disconnected the call.

Adriane walked down the hall to her bedroom where she removed her clothes and headed for the bathroom to take a shower when her phone rang again.

Adriane thought about letting it go to voicemail, but decided to answer the call.

"Is this the coward again?" Adriane asked as she answered the phone.

"Adriane."

"Yes."

"This is officer Stanley. I was at your home yesterday."

"Okay, what can I do for you?"

"Have you been on the phone?"

"Yes."

"Why?"

"We've been monitoring your calls and almost had a trace on your last call. Was that call from someone you know?"

"No, it was that fucking coward."

"You mean the one that's been threatening you?"

"Yes."

"Okay, the next time they call, keep them on the phone as long as you can so we can get a trace on his or her location."

"Okay, I will."

"My partner and I are sitting right outside."

"Whoever it was, knows you're here."

"That's good. That means they won't try anything since they know we are here."

"I'm getting ready to take a shower and if I get any more calls from this person, I will be sure to keep them on the phone as long as I can."

"Okay, and give me a call at the number I gave when you're finished showering."

"Sure will."

Adriane disconnected the call and placed her phone on the bathroom counter as she got into the shower.

Twenty minutes later, Adriane grabbed a towel, wrap it around her body and went into the bedroom where she dries off and lotions her body. She then grabbed a pair of sweatpants and a shirt and put it on. She just happened to remember to call officer Stanley to let him know she was finished showering.

Adriane walked back into the bathroom to grab her phone that she laid on the bathroom counter, but it wasn't there. Adriane looked on the floor and on the side of the toilet in case it fell, but it wasn't there. Adriane knew she placed it on the counter, but just in case she didn't she went back to the bedroom to check. She checked all over the room, but still no phone. Adriane was headed down the hall to go out the door to where the police were to let them know she was out of the shower when her phone rang. Adriane followed the sound of her phone ringing in the kitchen and there it was sitting right on the kitchen table.

Adriane picked up the phone. "Hello." But all she could hear was laughter.

Adriane froze in her tracks. She now knew this person was in the house while she was showering.

Adriane dropped her phone, ran to the door and when she opened the door, officer Stanley was standing there.

"I was coming to check on you."

"That person was in here."

"What!"

"Right after I spoke with you, I laid my phone on the bathroom counter, but when I finished showering, my phone was gone. I was on my way to tell you I was finished when my phone rang and I found it in the kitchen."

"Are you sure you didn't leave it in the kitchen?"

"Yes, I am sure. I was standing in the hall between the bedroom and bathroom when I was speaking with you. I didn't go to the kitchen I went straight into the bathroom. And when I answered my phone, they just laughed like the joke was on me and if they were in here, it was on me."

"Stay right here. I want to check the house."

"Don't forget to check the basement."

After searching the house, they didn't find anyone, but they found a way the person may have entered.

"I found a small window in the basement that was unlocked so I locked it back. That could have been an entryway if someone was in here."

"We're going to stay here inside with you until Mr. Stevens gets home if that's okay with you."

"Sure have a seat and make yourselves comfortable. I was just about to fix some lunch. Would you guys care to join me?"

"Yes, we would love to."

ENVY

CHAPTER TWENTY-FIVE

"I can't believe someone was in here right up under your nose. Do I need to hire someone to keep her safe since you guys can't do your damn job!" Drake shouted. He was so infuriated with the two police officers.

"Drake, it's okay. It's not their fault. Whoever it was came through one of the windows in the basement from the back."
"That's it, I didn't want to do this, but this person leaves me with no choice."

"What are you talking about?"

"I'm getting you a gun and I am going to teach you how to shoot it."

"Drake, I don't want a gun. You know how bad my temper is." Adriane pleaded with Drake about not getting a gun.

"Look, Adriane, I can't be with you 24/7. I would feel much better knowing that when I am not around, you will have something to protect you."

"You think a gun is going to protect me."

"Is there any way she can stay with some family members until this person is caught?" One of the police officers asked. Drake stood looking out the living room window with his back to the officers.

"I guess that's possible," Drake said as he turned around to look at Adriane.

"No, I am not leaving my home because of some asshole."

"Adriane right now is not the time to be brave. You have to be smart right now. This person was in the house and you didn't even know it."
Adriane paced back and forth with her hand on her hip.

"I don't know Drake. I can't let this person tear us apart and if I go back home, that's what this person will be doing."
"Just think about it, okay?" Drake asked.

Later that evening, while Adriane was in the kitchen cooking dinner, Drake was on the phone with John.

"Man, I can't believe this person was inside the home. The person has gone too far." John said.

"I know. I'm so mad right now I can't even see straight."

"I think it is time to pay Pete a visit," Drake said.

"Do you think it's him?"

"I don't know, but I will definitely find out. You can trust me on that."

"Maybe we need to make that visit together," John said.

"Let's do it."

"I'll meet you at your parents in an hour or so," Drake said.

"Okay, later," John said.

After dinner, Drake dropped Adriane off at her parents while he and John took a little trip to see Pete.

When the two arrived at Pete's, they saw him in back washing his car. The two pulled up on him and hopped out before Pete had a chance to do anything. By the time Pete saw the two, it's too late.

Pete tried to run, but John blocked his path as Drake moved in on him.

Drake punched Pete in the mouth. "You bitch ass nigga."

"Man, I sorry. I didn't mean to shoot you, I was scared."

Drake pulled Pete up by the collar with both hands. "Let's take a ride," Drake whispered in his ear.

The two men escorted Pete back to Drake's truck. Drake got in and John opened the door for Pete to get in and then John got in after him.

"Where are we going and what are you two going to do to me?"

"Don't worry, I'm not going to hurt you," Drake said as he grinned.

Twenty minutes later, they pulled into a secluded area in the park.

Drake cut the engine and sat there a minute before getting out. Drake walked around to the passenger side of the car. Pete was still sitting inside.

"Get out!" Drake yelled.

"Please man, don't hurt me."

"I said get out! Don't make me pull your ass out."

Pete slowly got out of the truck. He had no idea what was getting ready to happen.

Once he got out, Drake grabbed a hold of him and slammed him against the truck and gave him an uppercut to the stomach and a left jab to the face. Pete slid down to the ground.

"Now that's for shooting me, you punk ass."

John pulled Pete up off the ground and stood him up.

"I'm going to ask you some questions and I want you to be truthful to me and I promise if you are, nothing else will happen.

Did you throw a brick through Drake and Adriane's place the other night?"

"What! No, I did no such thing."

"Were you at their house today while my sister was taking a shower and have you been calling her threatening her?"

"No, I swear. I would never hurt Adriane. I care about Adriane. I could never do anything to hurt her." Pete said as he looked over at Drake.

"I'm sorry Drake, but I still have feelings for her, and I probably always will, but I would never do anything to harm her. You got to believe me."

Drake and John looked at each other. Drake walked around to the driver's side of the car and got in. John opened the passenger door and signaled for Pete to get in.

The ride back to Pete's was quiet. Drake and John wrecked their brain trying to figure out who could be behind this if it wasn't Pete, but they continued to draw a blank.

Once Adriane and Drake made it back to their place, as soon as they pulled into the driveway, Adriane sees the red paint splattered on the front door.

"Oh my God! Look at that." Adriane shouted.

Drake hopped out of the car. "Stay here," Drake yelled to Adriane.

Drake ran up to the porch and then ran to the back of the house to see what was going on back there.

Adriane got out of the car and walked around to the back. She stood as she watched Drake check out the back of the house.

"See if you would have installed those security cameras, we would know who was behind this." Frustrated, Adriane walked back around to the front of the house and took a seat on the top step as she waited for Drake before entering the home.

"Babe you're right. I should have had the cameras installed."

"Drake, it almost seems as though you don't want to know who's behind this. All it would haven taken was to have those cameras installed and boom we could have seen who was doing this. I'm so confused right now." Adriane said as she stood.

"I can't believe you said that."

"Whatever, Drake I am too tired to argue with you," Adriane said as she unlocked the front door and walked in.

"Can you do me a favor and check the basement window and make sure it is still locked? Thank you!" Adriane said as she made her way down the hall to the bedroom.

Drake came up from the basement and went to find Adriane.

"The windows were locked and nothing looks out of the ordinary. I'm not going into work tomorrow. I am going to work from home after I install the cameras. I know, I should have listened to you and I'm sorry babe."

Adriane walked over to Drake. "You know a hard head makes for a soft behind, right."

"Yes, how many times have I heard that as a child, now I'm hearing it as an adult, but I guess I deserve it."

"Yes, you do. This just tells me that if our baby takes after you, I will have two hard heads on my hand." Adriane laughed as she playfully swatted at Drake.

"I have never heard you complain about my hard head so why complain now?"

Adriane rolled her eyes at Drake. You make me sick."

"Really, well, why don't you let me make you feel good."

"Drake, is that all you think about?"

"I can't help it that pregnant pussy is so damn good."

"Oh, so are you saying that if I wasn't pregnant, it wouldn't be so damn good? As I recall, I had no complaints from you or anyone else for that matter."

"Don't go there Dri."

"No, don't you go there. My shit is good whether I'm pregnant or not."

"I didn't mean it like that."

Adriane laughed. "I know. I just like messing with you. I love getting those drawls in a knot."

"Just like I love getting yours off," Drake said as he grabbed hold of Adriane and backed her up to the bed and slowly lay her down.

Drake pulled his shirt off and unfastened his pants while Adriane lay there in awe of her man.

"Do you see anything you like?" Drake asked.

"Naw, not really," Adriane said.

"Well, if that's the case, let me put my shirt back on," Drake said as he bent over to pick up his shirt.

"Boy, stop playing."

"I told you about that boy shit."

Adriane moved off the bed and stood. She began undressing as Drake stood there. She took her shirt off and unfastened her bra.

"Damn, them tits are getting big. Just like I like them." Drake said as he moved closers, bent down and took a nipple into his mouth.

"Um daddy, that feels good."

"I have something else that's going to make you feel good." Drake ran his tongue across the nipple as his hand massages the other nipple.

Adriane reached for his manhood and pulled it out. She began to run her finger across the tip of it as her mouth watered at the thought of having her lips wrapped around it.

"All right baby girl, do your thing," Drake said as he could tell the need for her to wrap her lips around him.

Adriane slowly dropped to her knees. She grabbed a hold of him and began to lick each side of him. Then she licked the tip before taking the head into her mouth. She slowly inched him further and further into her mouth until he disappeared. She took him in and out and licked each side of him as her hand massaged the base of him.

"Damn, I love it when you suck me off like a Popsicle." Drake's legs began to wobble. He reached down and pulled Adriane up and laid her on the bed. He pulled her sweats off and then her panties. She spread her legs for him because she knew what time it was, it was all you can eat at the buffet.

Denise Hill

CHAPTER TWENTY-SIX

The next morning, Drake installed two cameras just like he promised. He installed one in the front of the house and one in the back. The one in the back was installed on the fence and it looked like a squirrel to throw intruders off and the one in the front looked like a light

Later that afternoon Drake set up shop in his office. Just as he promised Adriane, he was working from home.

Drake was busy on the computer when he heard a knock at the door. Drake looked up to see Adriane standing.

"Hey babe, what's up?"

"Since you're busy working, I thought I would go by to see Mother Brown. I want to talk to her about some things."

"Do you want me to go with you?"

"No, you go ahead and finish what you're doing. I'll be fine," She said as she walked further into the office over to Drake. She bent down and kisses him on the forehead.

"I won't be too long. I will pick up some dinner for us as well. Do you have anything in particular that you want?"

"No, not really."

"Okay, if you change your mind, just call me," She said as she turned to leave.

"Hey, make sure you watch your surroundings."

"Okay, babe."

As Adriane pulled up to Mother Brown's she noticed that Megan's car was nowhere around.

Adriane got out and walked up to the house. She rang the doorbell twice before the door opened.

"Hey, baby. How are you?" Mrs. Brown asked.

"I'm good. How are you?"

"I'm doing okay. I'm just sitting here watching a little TV."

"I stopped by because I wanted to talk to you about some things."

"Okay, come on into the family room and make yourself comfortable. Can I get you something to drink or to eat?"

"Oh no, I'm fine."

Mrs. Brown took a seat on the couch next to Adriane. Mrs. Brown picked up the remote control and turned the volume down.

"So what's on your mind sweetheart?"

"Well, you know the last time Drake and I was over here we told you that someone had broken into our basement and that someone had hit me in the head and knocked me out. We are continuing to have these incidents and now we are starting to get threatening phone calls. I believe someone wants to make sure I don't have this baby."

"Oh my God!" Mrs. Brown said as she lifted her hands to cover her mouth.

"The police have gotten involved. They may come over here and talk to you guys about some things especially Megan."

"Now I hope you don't think Megan is involved."

"She's a suspect seeing that I am with Drake and is carrying his child. Do you happen to know where Megan is?"

"Yes, I do. Your father took her to get a rental car while her car is being worked on."

"I just wanted to give you a heads up on what's going on."

"Are there any other suspects, because I don't believe Megan would do anything to harm you or that baby. I know how she feels about Drake, but Megan wouldn't do anything like this."

"I hope not because I would hate to see her behind bars or somewhere else."

"I will talk with Megan when she gets back and then I will call you."

Mrs. Brown grabbed Adriane's hand. "Baby please be careful and if I can do anything, please let me know."

Adriane looked into Mrs. Browns eyes and sees the sincerity.

"I will."

Adriane continued to sit and chat with Mrs. Brown. She was trying to wait for Megan to get home, but her stomach started to growl so she decided to head to the grocery store before heading home.

Adriane pulled away as she waved goodbye to Mrs. Brown, who was standing in the doorway.

Adriane drive down the street listening to 96.3 bobbing her head to the sounds of Chris Brown's "Fine China," she stopped at the four- way stop when someone rear-ended her from behind. Adriane put the car in park and waited for the driver to get out, but instead the driver just sat there. Adriane got out and was walking to the back of her car to see if there is any damage when the car pulled off, she tried to see who was driving, but the driver had on a black ski mask. Adriane hopped back into her car and called Drake. Panic set in as she tried to dial his number, but she continued to dial the wrong number. So she decided to drive home.

As Adriane pulled off and turned left onto 62nd street, she drove a mile before noticing the same car behind her again. Adriane sped up and so did the car behind her. She made a quick right, but the car kept up with her. She sped up trying to lose the car, but unfortunately, the car stayed on her tail and all at once, the car rear-ended her car so hard that it knocked her into the other lane and into a ditch. Adriane hit her head, the airbag exploded, hitting her in the chest and part of her stomach.

Adriane laid in the ditch unconscious as the rescue squad arrived.

It took the rescue squad about thirty minutes to get her out. She was bleeding from her head and nose and once they realize she was pregnant, they started to worry about the baby.

Drake checked his watch twice before calling Adriane. The first time he called it rang several times and then it went to voicemail. The second time he called, and an unfamiliar voice answered.

"Hello, who is this?"

"This is a member of the rescue squad."

"Rescue squad. Has there been an accident involving Adriane Pruett?"

"Yes, there has been. We just cut her out of the car and will be heading to Community North Hospital.

"Is she alive?"

"Sir, you can meet us there."

Drake turned off the computer locked up and jumped in his truck. He was running red lights trying to get to the hospital as quick as possible.

Drake arrived just as they were bringing Adriane in. He was running toward her, calling her name when one of the nurses stopped him and guided him to the nurse's stations.

"Let them work on her while you sit here and give me some information on her."

"Is the baby alive?"

"I don't know all the details, but I know she will be okay. She's unconscious right now."

Drake covered his face with his hands as he broke down.

"Sir, does she have any other family members that you need to notify?"

Drake got up and walked away. He pulled out his cell phone and called the Oliver's and the Browns and in no time, both families were there except for Megan.

The Oliver's were very standoffish toward the Browns and considered their family to be higher on the list than they were.

"When can we speak with the doctor?" Mrs. Oliver asked.

"Is the baby okay?" Mrs. Brown asked.

"I don't know. I don't know anything yet," Drake said in frustration.

An hour later, the doctor made his way to the waiting area.

"Is the family of Adriane Pruett here?"

"Yes, we're here," Mrs. Oliver and Drake said as the rest of the family moved closer to the doctor.

"Is Adriane and the baby okay?" Drake asked.

The doctor looked at Drake. "Yes, they are, thank God. This could have turned out much worse. Adriane has a concussion and the baby is fine. Adriane will experience some soreness in her chest and she hit her head so she had a gash that we stitched up, but other than that, she should be fine."

"Can I see here?" Drake asked.

"Yes, I will walk back with you."

"I wanted to speak to you in private. She said someone deliberately rear-ended her and caused her to go into the ditch. So I notified the authorities. They should be here shortly."

"Thank you, sir," Drake said as he shook the doctor's hand. Drake made his way inside Adriane's room. When he walked in he found her staring at the ceiling.

"Hey, how do you feel?" Drake asked as he walked up to her bed.

"Drake someone tried to kill me."

"Are you sure?"

"Yes, I am sure. When I left Mother Brown's the car rear-ended me slightly and then whoever was driving took off and as I was driving down 62nd street, the car came upon me again and hit me from behind, but this time it was much harder." Drake was just about to ask her more details when the door opened and in walked two police officers.

Adriane and Drake watched as the police officers made their way further into the room.

"Adriane Pruett?"

"Yes, that's me."

"We have a few questions for you if you don't mind."

"No, not at all."

The first police officer walked over to the right side of her and the other one stood at the left side of her.

"Now you told the doctor that someone deliberately ran you into a ditch?"

"Yes. The first time the car rear-ended me while I was at a four- way stop. I got out and the driver pulled off and as I made it further down the street and made a left turn on E 62nd

street, the same car rear-ended me again causing me to go into the other lane and into the ditch."

"Were you able to get a good look at the driver?"

"I didn't, but whoever it was, wore a black ski mask."

"Can you describe the car?"

"All I know is that it was a blue SUV, maybe an Envoy."

"We have had some incidents at our house. You can contact these people they know all about it?" Drake said as he handed the police officer one of the police officers cards.

"That's all for right now, but we will be in touch." The second officer said.

"The Oliver's and the Brown's are out in the waiting area. I know they are desperately waiting to get in here. I'll go and bring them back." Drake said.

"Okay, babe."

Drake walked back to the waiting area, but on his way back, he thought about calling his boy's from the day to get involved, but he wanted to speak to Adriane about this because once they got involved, it could get real ugly."

ENVY

CHAPTER TWENTY- SEVEN

Adriane was released the next day from the hospital. She was a little nervous about returning home. She only wished she was not pregnant so she wouldn't be putting her baby in harm's way.

"Man, I wish I wasn't pregnant right now because I would go and hunt that motherfucker that ran me off the road."

"Once we get inside, I want to talk to you about something." Adriane and Drake make it inside. Drake guided Adriane to the couch and he took a seat right next to her.

"I want to get your okay on this before I get some people involved. I have some friends I can call who can handle the situation, but it could get real ugly and if they get caught, it could come and bite me in the ass."

"No, Drake. I don't want you getting into any trouble over this. Let's just let the police handle this. I'll even allow you to get me a gun and if something happens and I kill this person, it will be on me, it will be self- defense."
Drake sat for a minute with his head down.

"Okay, I will get you a gun, but I can't promise you that if anything else happens, I won't hesitate to get my boys involved." Drake got up and walked out the door and stood on the porch.
As he paced back and forth, he noticed a car pulling up. He didn't recognize the car so he pulled out his gun and made his way off the porch and slowly walks to the car when he sees it's Megan.
Megan gets out furious. "Why in the world would your girlfriend tell my mother that I'm harassing her and shit?"

"Are you behind the incidents that have happened," Drake asked as he put his gun back in the back of his pants.
Adriane was inside and heard a female voice. She got up off the couch and made her way to the door. When she sees Megan, her blood began to boil. Adriane walked quickly out the door

and headed down the steps when she sees Drake's gun in the back of his pants. She walked over and pulled it from his pants and before Drake could react, she had the gun pointed at Megan's head.

"You want me and my baby out of the way bitch. Well here's your chance." She said as she removed the gun from Megan's head and handed her the gun. "Now go ahead and do it, because the next time you try something, I promise, I will blow your fucking brains out.

Drake grabbed the gun from Adriane's hand. "Megan get out of here."

"I'm sorry Adriane, but I am not the one who wants you dead. Who else hates you as much as I do?"

Adriane and Drake stood there as Megan pulled out of the driveway. Adriane turned to Drake, "If it wasn't her, then I have no idea who it could be."

"Maybe it's someone who you would least expect it to be."

"I know it couldn't be Pete."

"No, it's not him. He still has the hots for you."

"And how do you know that?"

"Don't worry about how I know. Just know that I know." Drake said as he started laughing.

"Come on, let's get back inside and try to piece things together."

Once inside, the two wrecked their brain trying to figure it out. Is it possible that Renee could secretly hate you?"

"Is it possible that she wants you?"

"No, that's not possible," Drake said.

"Then it's not possible that she secretly hates me. Oh my God! Why didn't I think of this? It's Sharon."

"Sharon."

"Yes. Renee said after she found out about us and we fought, she was livid. Renee said she had never seen her that angry."

"If it's her we need proof. Right now we have nothing that leads back to her."

"Let's check the cameras to see if anyone has been here." Drake and Adriane head into the office. Drake flipped the light switch, walked over to his desk and pulled his chair out for Adriane to sit in. He turned on his computer in his office as they watched for any activity while they were away.

"Oh my God! Who is that? It looks like two figures." Adriane said as she places her hand over her mouth.

"Let me try and zoom in a little closer," Drake said. Drake leaned back in the chair as they watch two people on the video.

"Drake we need to show this to the police. They need to know that it's not just one person." Adriane said. Drake continued to sit without saying a word. He couldn't believe what he was seeing. Drake rubbed his hand over his face, then he pulled out his phone and called officer Stanley.

Twenty minutes later, Drake and Adriane heard a knock at the front door.

"Stay here, I'll get it," Drake said. Drake walked to the front door to see two officers standing there. He didn't recognize either one of them.

"Can I help you guys?" Drake asked.

"Yes, officer Stanley sent us over here to view some video footage. I'm officer Smith and my partner is officer Jones."

"Okay, come on in." Drake opened the door and allowed the officers to come in. You can follow me."

Drake led them into his office. "Officer Smith and officer Jones, this is my fiancée Adriane Pruett."

"Nice to meet you. Officer Stanley has filled us in on the case." Officer Jones said.

"Great. So will you guys be on the case from now on?" Adriane asked.

"Yes, we will." Officer Smith said. "Officer Stanely has been assigned to another case.

"Well, this is what we capture while we were out," Drake said.

"We thought it was just one person responsible, but now we know it's two people."

"It looks like a male and female if you ask me." Officer Jones said.

"But they are not doing anything. If we could verify who they are, we could only get them for trespassing."

"What!" Adriane asked.

"They haven't broken any other law."

"Um… this is just too much for me right now. I think I need to take a nap." Adriane said showing her frustration.
Adriane walked out and made her way down the hall to the bedroom.

Later that evening, while Drake and Adriane went to dinner, Megan sat parked in her driveway for hours. She couldn't believe Adriane would think she would go out of her way to hurt her. True enough, she hated her for being with Drake and carrying his child, but after all, she was her sister. They shared the same blood and she would never hurt anyone in her family.
Megan pulled out of the driveway and drove around for thirty minutes until it was dark. She parked down the street from Drake's and watched as the two returned home from dinner. She was just about to pull off when she noticed a blue SUV slow down as it crept closer to the house.
Megan slid down in her car to keep from being seen. The driver made a U- turn and drove into the woods that was on Drake's property.

"What is this person up to," Megan said. Megan continued to sit and watch until this person was out of sight. She decided to follow this person to see who it was and what they were up to.
Megan got out of her car and made her way into the woods.
Megan was deep into the woods when she sees a shadow.
Megan quickly hides behind a tree as the person walked past

her. She watched as this person goes back to their truck, pulled out a shovel and walked back.

Megan moved around the tree to keep from being seen, but in doing so, she stepped on a branch which caused a noise.

The intruder stood and looked around the woods and when Megan peeked around the tree she was face to face with the person. The last thing she remembered was seeing a shovel coming down, hitting her in the face knocking her out.

The intruder dropped the shovel, grabbed a hold of Megan's arms and pulled Megan's body back to the truck and put her in the trunk.

The intruder goes back to get the shovel, threw it in the back of the truck with Megan and backed out of the woods.

Hours later, Megan awoke tied to a bed in a dark room. She heard music coming from outside the room to mask a conversation going on with a female and a male.

"What are you going to do with her. I thought the plan was to get Adriane. What does Megan have to do with this?" The male asked.

"She has everything to do with it. She was trying to play I Spy and would have gone straight to the police if I had not heard her."

"But she can't stand Adriane."

"I know, but they are sisters and blood is thicker than water."

"So what's the plan now?"

"We will have to get rid of both sisters."

"No!" Megan says under her breath. As she tried to get loose. She had ropes tied to both wrists and ankles. She moves her head to the side and that's when she felt the excruciating pain at the top of her head. She screamed out in pain.

"Ouch! Somebody help me!" She screamed as she tried to get loose.

Megan reached over to her wrist and tried to untie the knot with her teeth, the knot was almost untied, but when she heard someone turn the doorknob, Megan quickly laid her head down on the pillow and pretended to be asleep.

A tall person with a black ski mask on their face walked over to her to see if she was awake and when he seen she was still out, he turned to leave.

"See, you're paranoid. She's still out like a light." The man said.

" I know I heard someone scream." The female said as she walked into the room and looked at Megan.

"How could you have heard her with the music up so loud?"

"I have good ears,"

"Apparently not."

"Well, let's give her this just to make sure she stays out until we decide what to do with her." The female said as she pulled out a syringe and injected Megan in the side of her neck.

Denise Hill

CHAPTER TWENTY-EIGHT

The next morning, Officer Smith and Officer Jones drove by Drake's and found an abandon parked car a couple of houses down from Drake's. The officers got out and check out the car. The doors were locked so they couldn't get inside so they ran the plates and traced it back to the Enterprise rental car company. After researching, they find out that the car was rented to a Megan Brown.

They got the address and headed over to talk to Megan Brown. The officers arrived at the Brown's expecting to see Megan, but when they get there, they find out that Megan didn't come home last night. Mr. & Mrs. Brown were very worried about their daughter.

"When's the last time you saw your daughter?" Officer Smith asked.

"I saw her last around 6 pm yesterday evening. She sat in the driveway for hours listening to music in her car." Mr. Brown said.

"When did you realize she was gone?" Officer Jones asked.

"I went outside to get her for dinner around 6:30 and that's when I noticed she was gone." Mrs. Brown said.

"Does she have a boyfriend or any friends she may be staying with?"

"No, she doesn't have a boyfriend and we have already check with her friends and no one has seen her."

"We found her car abandoned over by Sargent Road. Is there any reason why she would have been over there?" Mr. & Mrs. Brown looked at each other.

"She and Drake Stevens used to date and now he's dating her sister."

"Um… And how does Megan feel about that?" Officer Jones asked.

"She's not happy about it."

"So it Adriane your daughter?" Officer Jones asked.

"Yes, it's a long story, but yes, she is our daughter also." Mrs. Brown said.

"Are you guys aware of some of the incidents that have been happening over at Drake's?"

"Yes, we are aware of that. My daughter Adriane stopped by the other day to talk with me about it."

"Does she believe Megan is involved?"

Mrs. Brown hesitated before answering. "I assured her that Megan would never do anything to harm her."

"You didn't answer my question."

"I think she believes Megan is involved, but Megan is not. I promise she's not involved."

"What do you mean? How do you know she's not involved?"

"Because I know my daughter, officer." Mrs. Brown said.

"If Megan does show up, can you contact us. We want to talk with her and if she doesn't show up within the next 24 hours, you might want to file a missing person report." Officer Smith said.

The officer handed Mrs. Brown his card with his phone number on it.

Megan opened her eyes to see a female standing over here. She couldn't make out who this person was because her vision was a little blurry from the drug that was injected into her neck.

"Why are you doing this to me?"

"This is what happens when you are a nosey ass. I have no issues with you, but when you decided to show up at Drake's and you saw us, I had no choice, but to bring you here."

The female's voice sounds familiar to Megan. "Who are you? Do I know you?"

"There you go being nosey again."

"Your voice sounds familiar to me."

"It should, you've been in my way for years."

"What do you mean?" Megan asked as she tried to move her arms.

"I'm talking about Drake. You were always hanging around always on his dick."

"Drake was my boyfriend. What did you expect me to do?"

"You didn't deserve Drake and neither does that bitch ass sister of yours."

Megan turned to face the female. "Sharon I can't believe you're the one behind this. You are the one that's been harassing Adriane and making everyone believe it was me. You stupid bitch, you will never get away with any of this."

"Oh, but I will. You just said I have everyone believing it was you that's been harassing her."

"Yeah, but when I don't show up, people will look for me and know that I am not involved. You're so dumb."

Sharon walked over to Megan and slapped her hard.

Megan laughed. "Is that all you got?"

Sharon rushed over and wrapped both hands around Megan's throat.

"Keep fucking with me," Sharon shouted!

The male sitting in the living room heard the commotion and walked back to the room to see what's going on.

He ran over and grabbed Sharon. "What the hell are you doing?" He asked as Megan tried to get her breath.

"This little bitch here was pissing me the fuck off."

"We need to stick to the plan."

The male pulled Sharon to the side. "I didn't get involved in this to go to jail, but if you continue to lose your cool, that's what's going to happen."

"Oh, don't worry Pete, you will have your precious Adriane in due time." She said knowing good and well she had plans of her own to kill Adriane. She can't let her live knowing she's carrying her man's baby and since Megan is here, she will kill her as well and if Pete's gets in the way, she will take him out also.

Sharon left Pete in the room with Megan. He walked over and closed the door halfway. "Pete is that you?"

Pete looked over at Megan. "You can't let her do this. She is planning on killing Adriane and me. You have got to stop her Pete. You're not a killer." Megan pleaded with Pete.

Pete stopped, turned around and looked at the door. He walked over and closed the door.

"What do you mean she's planning to kill Adriane?"

"She told me she was going to kill her and if you got in the way, she would take you out as well. You've got to get me out of here."

Pete stood in silence for a minute and then he moved over to the headboard where Megan's wrists were tied and started to untie her.

"I want you to get out of here and go warn Adriane and remember I helped you."

"You really love her, don't you?"

"Yes, I do."

Once Megan was loose, Pete helped her up, but before Megan had a chance to escape, Sharon walked in on them with a gun in hand.

"What the fuck are you doing Pete!"

"I can't let you hurt Adriane. Megan told me how you were planning to kill her."

Sharon looked at Megan and tried to pass Pete to get to her. "No, Sharon stop!" Pete yelled.

Pete and Sharon wrestled. "Get out of here Megan," Pete shouted.

Megan headed for the door, but just as she did, the gun went off. Megan didn't look back, she continued running to the front door. She removed the chain and unlocked the deadbolt and was out of the house in no time.

Megan continued to run down the street until she ran upon some young boys.

"Please help me. Someone is trying to kill me." She said as she grabbed onto the biggest guy.

"Who's trying to kill you?" He asked as Megan looked up to see Sharon running down the street after her.

"She is. Help me!"

The guys gathered in front of Megan as Sharon ran up to them. They pull out their weapons just as Sharon approached.

"Drop your gun and there won't be any problems."

Sharon came to a halt. She didn't want any beef with these guys. She lowered her weapon and backed away from them. "I don't want any trouble with you guys. I'm lowering my gun." She said as she continued backing away from them. When she got so far, she turned and ran back to the house.

The men put their weapon up and turned to face Megan. "Everything's good Lil momma." The youngest guy said. "Do you need a ride somewhere?"

Megan was hesitant to say yes, but she felt safer with them than by herself.

"Yes, I do. I need a ride home if you don't mind."

"What's your name shawty?" One of the guys asked as they walked her to their car.

"My name is Megan Brown."

"So how did you get involved with Blondie Megan Brown?" One of the guy's asked, referring to Sharon as Blondie because of her blonde hair.

"She's trying to kill my sister because my sister is pregnant and engaged to a guy that she used to mess with."

"Damn, Blondie is off the chain. You and your sister better be careful."

"Oh, we will." At this moment, Megan felt sorry for how she had treated Adriane. As she rode home, she thought about what Adriane may have gone through as a child and this made her feel even worse.

Twenty minutes later, the car pulled up in front of the Brown's.

Before getting out, Megan thanked the guys for saving her life and giving her a ride home.

Megan jumped out the car and ran up to the house. Mrs. Brown heard a car pulling up and was on her way to the door when she sees Megan.

"Oh my God! Megan where have you been?" Mrs. Brown asked as Megan broke down crying in her arms.

"Megan calm down and tell me what happened."
By this time, Mr. Brown was standing at the door and walked out to hug his daughter and bring her inside.

"Sharon is trying to kill Adriane. She hit me in the head and she and Pete had me tied up at some old boarded up house. She's going to kill Adriane. She shot Pete because he helped me to escape. We have got to call the police and warn Drake and Adriane.

Later that night, after the police had stopped by to let them in on what was going on. Drake and Adriane had just finished eating dinner when they heard a loud sound outside the house. Drake walked to the front door and saw the police car parked at the end of their driveway. Officer Jones waved and got back into the car where they would be stationed until the morning.

"You know I would never have thought that Sharon and Pete would be working together to kill me," Adriane said as she flopped down onto the couch.

"Well, like Megan said, Pete had no intentions of killing you that was Sharon's thinking."

"But still, to kill me over a guy who has no interest in you. I don't understand it."

ENVY

CHAPTER TWENTY NINE

That night, an APB was put out on Sharon. When Sharon ran out the house earlier after Megan, Pete was able to get out of the house through the back way and make his way to the hospital and was later in custody, but Sharon was still on the run.

They had her mother's house and the house she had taken Megan too under surveillance, but little did they know she was hiding out in Drake's basement.

Sharon knew once Megan got home, it wouldn't be too long before the police showed up to her mom's and to the place where she held her hostage. So she made her way over to Drake's because she knew no one would be looking for her there, but to her surprise, the police showed up just a little after she hid and was stationed out front.

They had a feeling she would eventually pay Drake and Adriane a visit and when she did, they wanted to be right there.

Inside the home, Adriane sat on the living room couch and looked out the window. She could see the parked police car out front, which made her feel a little better. Earlier, John and Mrs. Oliver tried to talk her into coming over there to stay with them, but she wanted to stay with Drake.

Down in the basement, Sharon paced back and forth trying to figure a way out without getting caught, but where would she go? She had no family outside of Indianapolis and she knew that if she showed up to her mom's home, her mom would make her leave or even worse, turn her in, but she couldn't leave without doing what she set out to do and that was to get rid of Adriane. If she left now, this would have all been for nothing.

Sharon was so busy pacing back and forth and thinking that she forgot where she was and screamed out loud because of her frustration and no sooner than the scream left her mouth, she regretted it.

Adriane still sitting on the couch, jumped when she thought she heard a scream. Drake, who was in the bedroom rushed out and into the living room.

"Are you okay?"

"Yes, who was was that?" Adriane asked

"I don't know. I thought that was you."

"No, it wasn't me." She said as she got up off the couch. "It sounded like it came from the kitchen or maybe even the basement."

Drake was just about to walk into the kitchen when they heard a knock at the front door.

"Stay back," Drake said as he walked to the door and opened it.

Drake slowly opened the door to find two police officers standing there with a surprised look on their faces.

"Is everything okay in here?" One of the police officers asked as Drake opened the door.

"Yes, we are fine, but we heard a scream that sounded like it came from our kitchen or either the basement."

The police officers entered the house and walked into the kitchen to look around. In the meantime, Sharon saw the two officers get out of the car and made their way to the house so she crawled through the basement window and ran deep into the woods.

After checking the kitchen, the officers decided to check the basement. The officer opened the basement door. "Is there a light switch on the wall?"

"Yes, but it's at the bottom of the stairs."

The police officers slowly made their way down the stairs until they came to the last step. The first police officer felt along the wall for the light switch. Once he found it, he flipped the switch. The two walked further into the basement when they heard a noise coming from over in the corner. They walked over to the corner with a gun in hand to find the basement window hitting up against the lock.

"Looks like whoever was down here got out through here." The officers locked the window and made their way back upstairs to the living room.

"Did you know your basement window was unlocked?"

"No, it shouldn't have been. I made sure it was locked when we got home."

"Well, it was unlocked. You might want to double check it just to make sure it's not broken."

Drake walked downstairs to the basement and walked over to the window with the first police officer behind him. Drake pushed on the window and it opened. He locked it back and pushed on it again and again it opened.

"You need something to secure this window until tomorrow," The police officer said.

"I know."

Drake looked around the basement for something, but he wasn't able to find anything, but some rope so he tied the rope around the lock and wrapped it around three or four times and then tied it in a knot.

"This should do until tomorrow," Drake said. "I will put a chair up against the basement door as well."

"Well, we will be parked out front so if you hear anything, just flick the lights and we will be right in."

Sharon found an old shed to hide inside for the night. She didn't want to return to the basement just yet. She tried to make herself comfortable, but she was cold and it was wet inside and it smelled. She would have given anything to be at home in her bed and under her covers where she would be nice and warm, but she had come too far to turn back and even if she decided to give up, she would be charged with kidnapping and attempted murder. Sharon was determined not to go to jail. She would end her life before she let that happened.

Adriane lay snuggled up to Drake as they talked about what was going on.

"You know this seems like a bad dream. I can't believe someone wants me dead."

"So you're telling me you had no idea Sharon was jealous of you?" "No, why would I. She never acted jealous in any way."

"I know I used to ask her about you all the time and she would get so mad. I would just laugh at her which made it worse."

"Why would you fuck someone and then ask them about another female. That's so not right."

"It wasn't like she was my girlfriend. It was just about sex and she knew that."

"No, she didn't. She thought it was more. That's why she wants to kill me. You meant so much more to her than you even know. You can't play with people's emotions. You men need to learn that. It can never be just about sex with a female unless she has someone already or if she's a hoe. I could never sleep around with someone if I didn't like them."

"Men do it all the time."

"Tell me about it. How many women have you slept with just for the sake of getting some?"

"Too many to count."

"I hope you used some protection."

"Of course. I used protection with Sharon. You and Megan are the only two that I didn't use any protection with and that was because I was serious with you two."

Adriane was quiet as she thought about what Drake had said about her and Megan. She hated that she and Megan would probably never be friends with each other because of Drake, but it wasn't like she set out to hook up with her sister's ex-boyfriend.

Adriane looked over at Drake, who had fallen asleep. She just stared at this man. She never thought she would find someone like him. Now she understands why Megan and Sharon were acting an ass over him. He is one hell of a catch that she planned to be with for the rest of her life and to have as many babies as he wanted.

Now she was so glad that she didn't get that job she applied for and she had decided to put school on hold until after the baby was born.

Right now, her focused was to stay alive and to have a healthy baby and to marry the man of her dreams.

Adriane continued to lay close to Drake as she fell into a deep sleep.

The next day, Drake went to the hardware store to talk to someone about getting his basement window replaced and then he returned home just in time to go to Adriane's doctor appointment.

Drake was so happy when he learned the sex of his baby and to actually see the ultrasound and hear the baby's heartbeat. He thought he would jump out of his pants when he heard the heartbeat and at the very moment, he only wished his parents were alive. He wanted to tell them the good news, but instead he phoned his sister and told her everything.

"Oh Drake, I am so happy for you. I can't wait to come home and meet Adriane. And I can't wait for my niece or nephew. I can't believe you won't tell me the sex."

"You just have to know everything don't you?"

"You know me."

"And that's why I am not telling you."

"What's Adriane's number?"

"Oh, No you won't." Drake laughed at his sister.

"What, I just want to talk with her and to congratulate her."

"Right. When are you coming home, sis?"

"I should be here another two months and then I will be home for at least a year and a half."

"That's so good to hear."

"Aw, so you miss your sister?"

"Yes, I actually do."

"I miss you too Drake. Well, let me get back to work and I will call you one day next week. Love you and give my love to Adriane."

"I will. Bye sis."

Drake missed his sister more than anything. After their parents died, it was just the two of them and they had become so close that he missed talking to her every day.

On the way home, Adriane wanted to stop at Baby's R Us to look at a baby bed.

"Man, these are nice."

"I know. There's so many to choose from. Which one do you like." Adriane asked Drake.

"I like all of them so anyone you pick will be good, but you know my baby girl has to have the best."

"Yes, I know that Drake," Adriane said as she walked over to Drake and kissed him on the lips. "Have I told you lately how much I love you?"

"Yes, but you can tell me again and again."

Denise Hill

CHAPTER THIRTY

The next couple weeks went by without any incidents. Adriane made several visits to Mother Oliver and to Mother Brown's. She felt it was only right to visit both women. Whenever she visited Mother Brown's she would always call a day in advance just to give Megan an opportunity to not be there. She had no problem visiting while Megan was there and on occasion, Megan would be there while she visited and they were cordial to each other.

Megan was still deeply in love with Drake and couldn't seem to shake it off. She tried everything to get him off her mind, but whenever she saw Adriane, it just brought up those feelings and it seemed to make her angry all over again. Mrs. Brown began to worry about Megan. She wasn't eating or sleeping. She had bags under her eyes and always seemed to be in a bad mood.

Mrs. Brown knocked at Megan's bedroom door. "Megan sweetheart, don't you want to come down and join us for dinner?"

"No, mom, I not hungry right now. If you can put me some food in the microwave, I will get it a little later."

"Well, can you at least come down and sit with us. Your dad and I want to talk to you about something."

"Sure mom, I will be down in a minute."

"Okay, sweetheart."

Minutes later, Megan came down to the kitchen and took a seat across from her mother.

"Honey, your dad and I are really worried about you. You don't eat or sleep. What can we do to help you?"

Tears began to roll down Megan's face. "Mom, I don't know what to do. I still love Drake. I can't get him off my mind. I don't know what to do or how I can go on."

"Aw, baby." Mrs. Brown said as she got up from the table and walked around to Megan and hugged her.

"Maybe you need to see a doctor. I think that would help."

"Maybe so," Megan said.

"I tell you what tomorrow I will call Doctor Scott and see if he can fit you in as soon as possible, okay."

"Okay, mom."

"In the meantime, you need to eat something." Mrs. Brown said as she got up, walked over to the microwave and warmed Megan's food up."

Adriane sat on the couch watching TV when she heard a loud noise. It sounded like glass breaking. Adriane looked outside and didn't see the police car that was parked out front. Drake was at work so she knew it wasn't him messing around outside.

Adriane got up off the couch, walked over to the front door, unlocked the screen and opened the door and stepped out onto the front porch. She walked over to the side of the porch and peered around the house, but didn't see or hear anything so she went back into the house.

Adriane locked the front screen and shut the storm door and when she turned around, Sharon was there to greet her. Adriane jumped, she wasn't expecting to see anyone, especially not Sharon.

"Sharon, what the hell are you doing here?" Adriane asked.

"Bitch don't worry about why I am here. You should be worried about what I plan to do." Just then, Sharon pulled out a gun.

"Now get your ass on the couch and sit down," Sharon said as she shoved Adriane to the couch.

"You know, if you didn't have that damn gun, I would beat the shit out of you."

"Well, why don't you pretend that I don't have it."

Both women looked at each and at the door when they heard someone turning the doorknob.

The door slowly opened and when it did, Drake stepped in.

"Drake she has a gun," Adriane yelled, but it was too late. Sharon was on Drake before he had a chance to do anything.

"Close the damn door and take a seat next to your bitch," Sharon said.

"I guess you two thought I had forgotten about you. No, I just wanted to let things die down before I made my next move."

"Are you okay?" Drake asked Adriane.

"Yes, I am fine."

"Sharon, what do you want with us?"

"You know damn well what I want. I want you and your baby."

"Don't you think it's a little too late for that and all? You know the police are still looking for you."

"Yes, I know that's why we have to make this quick. I haven't hurt anyone yet and if I'm pregnant, I know they will go easy on me. I will only do a short period of time and then we will be free to live our life together."

"Are you fucking crazy?" Adriane yelled.

"Yes crazy for this man here, but what I can't understand about him is why in the hell would he want to be with someone like you. What did you and Megan do to him that caused him to be so madly in love with you guys? Did you put a spell on him?"

"Do I look like I need to put a spell on anyone so they will be with me? No, that's some shit you would do."

Sharon moved to stand in front of Adriane. "You have one more time to say something slick and I promise I will bust you in your fucking face."

Drake moved closer to Adriane and covered her with his body.

"Oh, so you think you're protecting her. How about you do this." Sharon walked into the kitchen and pulled out one of the kitchen chairs.

"Tie your bitch to this chair here."

Drake hesitated. "Get the fuck up Drake," Sharon said as she waved the gun in the air. "And Adriane, close those blinds." After Drake tied Adriane to the chair. Sharon moved closer to him and grabbed him between the legs. I want some of this here and I want that skank to watch as we make love."

"Don't you dare touch him," Adriane yelled as she tried to get loose.

"Cover that bitches mouth," Sharon told Drake.

"If you want her mouth covered, then you will have to do it yourself."

"Get me some tape and don't try anything stupid Drake," Sharon said as she pointed the gun at Adriane's head.

After Sharon placed the tape across Adriane's mouth, she walked back over to Drake. "Unfasten your pants." She said. Drake gave Sharon an evil eye as he slowly unfastened his belt and then his pants.

"Pull your boxers down. I want to pleasure you right in front of your sweet Adriane."

Sharon grabbed a hold of Drake and began to massage him. She ran her tongue across the tip of his head and alongside him. She watched as he grew from pleasure. Sharon turned to look at Adriane. She wanted to get a reaction out of her.

"Damn, he is so big. I just love it when I come across a big dick. Don't you Adriane?"

Sharon could see the tears forming in Adriane's eyes. "He's going to fit perfectly inside me when I'm ready. What do you have to say about that, Adriane?"

Adriane continued to move trying to get loose.

With one hand, Sharon slid down her skirt along with her thong. She moved closer to Drake and pushed him back against the couch. She reached down and grabbed his hand and guided it to her vagina. "Touch me." She said. Drake hesitated, but thought about the consequences and moved his two fingers inside her as his thumb massaged her clit. "That's it, baby. Make me feel good."

Sharon began to move back and forth and all at once, she pulled his head to her. "It's dinner time." She said as she opened her legs wide while smiling and looking over at Adriane.

The smell of Sharon began to turn Drake on. He tried so hard to let his mind go somewhere else, but he couldn't. Drake ran his tongue up and down her and in and out of her vagina, which turned him on even more.

Meanwhile, Adriane cried as she tried to look away, but yet, still get untied.

"I swear, I am going to kill you." She said underneath the tape that covered her mouth.

Sharon looked at Drake and saw the want in his eyes. "Lay back," she said as she straddled him on the couch and took him in. She rode him seem like hours before he came, but when he came, it was so good he couldn't control himself because he continued to come and come.

"Damn baby, was I that good. I bet your girl over there has never made you come continuously, has she?

Hours later, Sharon was back at it. She continued to sex Drake until he became sore and swollen. "I'll let you rest for a while." She said as she walked over to Adriane and snatched the tape off of her mouth.

"Ouch!" Adriane yelled. "You think you're pretty smart, don't you."
Adriane asked.

"Yeah, I am. Let's see I fucked your man several times in front of you and you couldn't do anything about it in your own home and I plan to fuck him all night and make you watch. So I would say, yeah, I am pretty smart. I hoped to have his seed planted in me by the time I leave in the morning and if you're a good girl, I may just let you live."

"You're crazy as fuck," Drake said.

"And so is your sweet precious Adriane. I bet you didn't even know she's a stone cold killer. Did you?"

"What are you talking about?" Adriane yelled.

"Oh, you didn't think I knew you set your parents house on fire with them in it and that you cut Katie's brake line because you were mad because she caught you and Pete fucking and made you walk your little ass home after midnight."

"You have lost your damn mind," Adriane yelled.

"Oh, really. Too bad there's no evidence to put your ass behind bars."

"You're right, there is no evidence because it never happened you little stupid bitch," Adriane yelled as she got her left arm lose without Sharon noticing.

"Who are you trying to convince Adriane, me, Drake or yourself?"

"I'm not trying to convince anyone because I know better, but a bitch like you will always try and make someone else look bad because you do."

"Me, look bad, bitch never," Sharon said as she moved over to stand in front of Adriane.

"Drake, do I look bad? Do I taste or feel bad?"Sharon asked as she looked over at Drake.

"Just know while you were busy tasting my man, I hope you liked the taste of my ass and pussy on your lips hoe because that's where his dick has been. Now laugh about that shit." The way Adriane said this statement was too funny, Drake couldn't help but laugh and shake his head.

ENVY

CHAPTER THIRTY-ONE

Megan pulled into Drake's driveway. She had been pondering over this move for hours. She had to face her demon and at least try and move on with her life. Megan sat behind the wheel for a few minutes before getting out of the car. As she moved up the walkway, her surroundings felt a little eery. Megan stopped, looked around and listened before walking on. "It's just too quiet, something is not right, she said to herself.. Megan knocked on the door twice and no answer. She thought she heard movement inside, but no one came to the door. Megan knocked two more times, still no answer.

Megan turned to leave. She walked passed the two cars which told her that they were home. Then it dawned on her, what if Sharon had them held captive inside.

Megan went back to her car. She walked around to the passenger side of the car and opened the door. She opened the glove compartment and pulled out a flashlight and a revolver. Megan slowly made her way around to the back of the house where she sees the broken window. Megan crawled through the window and made her way up the stairs to the basement door that led to the kitchen. She listened before turning the knob and to her surprise, the door opened.

Megan was a little afraid to go in, she felt as though it was a trap so she stood there and tried to listen when she heard a female voice. It didn't sound like Adriane, but as Megan continued to listen she recognized the voice.

In the living room, Sharon was ready for another round with Drake.

"Drake, I want you to shower with me and then I'll be ready for another round of that crack."

Sharon, I have nothing else to give you. You've already drained me."

"Don't worry, I know there's plenty where that came from," Sharon said as she guided Drake down the hall to the bathroom with the gun pointed to his back.

As soon as Megan thought the coast was clear, she opened the basement door and eased inside. The kitchen was empty, so she moved further into the house when she saw Adriane in the living room tied to a chair.

Adriane saw something out of the corner of her eye move and when she turned, she saw Megan. Megan puts her finger up to her mouth for Adriane not to say a word.

Megan moved closer to Adriane and began to untie her.

"Hurry!" Adriane said.

"I'm moving as fast as I can," Megan said. Then the two heard the shower stop.

"They're coming," Adriane said. "Give me the gun, I am going to kill that bitch."

"No Adriane. You don't want to get in any trouble. You're pregnant, you will never survive in prison. Let me handle it."

Adriane didn't know if she should trust Megan or not.

"You can trust me, Adriane, I promise."

"Let's go and get help," Adriane said.

"No, I have all the help I need. Besides, that bitch hit me in my head. I got something for her ass."

Adriane and Megan walked quietly down the hall to stand in front of the bathroom door. Megan turned the knob and Adriane pushed the door opened to find Drake and Sharon having sex.

Adriane pushed Megan out of the way and ran to Drake and hit him from the back. "You son of a bitch."

Sharon looked up to see Adriane and to see Megan holding a gun pointed at her.

Adriane kicked the gun that was laying next to Sharon and pulled her out of the bathroom by her legs.

Adriane and Megan both started beating that ass. Drake was in shock to see both sisters working together.

Drake stood up, grabbed a hold of Adriane and pulled her out of the bathroom.

"Get your fucking hands off of me."

By this time, the police were outside when they heard the commotion on the inside. The two officers ran to the house, kicked the front door in and came running down the hall to find Megan and Sharon going at each other.

Megan was beating Sharon in the face with the butt of the gun.

"Ma 'am, put the gun down." The police shouted three times before shooting Megan in the arm.

"What the fuck! Why did you shoot her," Adriane yelled? This crazy bitch held us captive in our own home and you shoot my sister. Adriane was going after the cops when Drake pulled her back.

"You can't do this Adriane. Let them handle this."

Adriane breaks loose from Drake and runs to Megan's side. "You're going to be okay sis, just hold on."

Megan looked up at Adriane and smiled. "Can you believe this? We are at each other's side."

"That's what sisters are for," Adriane said as the tears rolled down her face.

Adriane looked over at Sharon and smiled. "That's what you get, you stupid bitch."

Sharon laughed. "That's okay, that's why I fucked your man right in front of you," Sharon said right before Adriane slapped the shit out of her.

Adriane rode to the hospital with Megan in the Ambulance. Adriane held onto Megan's hand.

"Just know I got your back, okay."

Megan looked up and smiled.

"Thank you, sis. I am so sorry for everything. If I could take it all back, I would, but I can't, I can only make things better going forward."

"And that's all I can ask of you."

Once they reached the hospital, they would not let Adriane go back to see Megan. She was being arrested along with Sharon until everything was cleared up.

Drake arrived at the hospital thirty minutes later, he was a little hesitant to come knowing Adriane was angry with him for enjoying the sexual escapade with Sharon.

Adriane was pacing back and forth when she looked up and see Drake walking in.

"What are you doing here?"

"I wanted to come and be with you."

"What the fuck for? You let it be known who you care about and it ain't me or this baby."

"Adriane, come on, don't act like this. What was I supposed to do? Let Sharon hurt or even kill you. I did what I had to do. Wouldn't you have done the same for me?"

"But I wouldn't have made it seem as though I enjoyed it as much as you did." She said as she rolled her eyes at him.

"I can't help it if I'm a good actor."

"Good actor my ass. You were not acting at all." She said as she got up to leave.

As Adriane was walking down the hall, Mr. & Mrs. Brown walked in.

"Adriane what are you doing here?"

"It's a long story." She said as she hugged both parents. They're not letting anyone see Megan because they placed her under arrest."

"My God! What happened." Mr. Brown asked. Adriane sat the couple down and told them the story.

"Well, at least something good came out of this." Mrs. Brown said.

"We need to get an attorney for Megan so they won't try and give her more time than she deserves."

"I know the perfect person." Mr. Brown said. My best friend's son is a criminal attorney. I will make a call to him right now."

"Are you sure Megan's okay?" Mrs. Brown asked.

"Yes, she's going to be okay."

"Are you and Drake okay?"

"I'm fine."

"What about Drake?"

"He couldn't be better."

Mrs. Brown could tell by Adriane's demeanor that something wasn't right.

"If you guys will excuse me, I need to make a phone call."

Adriane walked over to the corner, pulled out her phone and called John to come and pick her up from the hospital.

John arrived thirty minutes later. "Dang, what took you so long?"

"Adriane, I can't just stop everything for you when you call."

Adriane began to cry. She tried so hard to hold her feelings in, but what John said hurt her. He had always been there for her and never put anyone before her, but since she's been with Drake, things have changed. He wanted her to depend on herself or Drake.

"Come here. I didn't mean it like that, but you know you have a fiancé now and he may not like it, that you still depend on your brother instead of him."

Drake was still sitting waiting for Adriane to come back and when he heard John's voice, he walked around the corner to see what was going on. As soon as Drake turned the corner, John could sense something was wrong.

"Was going on Dri?"

"Sharon was at our house. She tied me up and had a gun on me. She made Drake have sex with her several times and from what I could tell, he enjoyed every bit of it."

John laughed. "What the fuck is funny?" Adriane asked.

"I'm sorry Dri, but what did you expect Drake to do?"

"I'm sorry I called you. I'll just walk the fuck home."

Adriane said as she headed for the elevators.

"Dri, stop being childish and think about the situation. I can't control my sexual feelings like that. I wish I could, but I

239

can't. I did not want to have sex with Sharon and you know it, but it was that or have her hurt you. I would do anything to protect you and that baby, but if I 'm wrong for that, then maybe we don't need to be together." Drake said as he hopped into the elevator.

"See Dri, you're wrong this time. Come on let me get you home."

Adriane walked over to the Browns and told them that she would call them in the morning.

When Adriane arrived home, she expected to see Drake, but Drake was nowhere in sight.

She walked into the kitchen and started preparing dinner. It was late, but she had not eaten since noon and she was starting to feel a little queasy. She knew Drake would be home soon and knew he would probably be hungry as well.

Drake sat at the bar drinking the night away. He was so hurt by Adriane's actions. He felt he did what any man would have done to protect the one's he loved, but he guessed that wasn't good enough for Adriane. He began to question her love for him and if he was really good enough for her.

Drake sat there and drank until the bartender cut him off.

"That's it buddy, no more alcohol for you tonight. Do I need to call you a cab?"

"No, I'm good," Drake said as he staggered out of the bar and onto the parking lot. Drake inserted his key into the lock, opened the door and hopped in. He laid his head back against the headrest and fell fast asleep. Drake awoke at 4 am. He looked around at his surroundings before he remembered that he was at Luke's.

Drake laughed. "Damn, I must have been really tired or really fucked up."

Drake said as he turned the ignition and reached for his phone to call Adriane, but the phone fall to the floor of the passenger side.

Drake pulled onto the street still searching for his phone and looked away for just a minute when he was hit by a semi head on.

FIVE MONTHS LATER

"Come on sis you can do it. Megan coached Adriane on while she was in the delivery room giving birth to her daughter Lake.

"Oh my God! She is killing me." Adriane cried out.

"She's coming I can see the head," Megan yelled.

"I'm an aunt," Megan shouted!

The Brown's and the Oliver's were so excited to see Lake make it into the world.

Adriane laid her head back on her pillow and cried. This was the happiest moment of her life. She only wished Drake could have been there to enjoy it with her.

Just then someone burst through the door with flowers and balloons.

"Where are my babies?" Drake asked. "Baby I am sorry, but I tried to get her as quick as I could."

THE END

COMING SOON....

THE MONITOR

CHAPTER ONE

"Okay sleepyhead, it's time to get up," Katie said as she entered her daughter's bedroom with Chole in her arms. She walked further into the room, bent over and kissed her daughter on the forehead.

Kelly turned over, rubbed her eyes and smiled when she sees her little sister.

"Did you sleep good?" Katie asked her daughter.

"No." She said groggily.

Katie laughed. "That's what you always say."

Kelly got out of bed and walked over to her mother. "Mom, can I hold her before I get dressed?

Katie handed the baby to Kelly.

"Hey, little one," Kelly said as she touched her sister's face with her finger. Chloe grinned and began to move as she was excited to see her big sister.

"Mom, is daddy still downstairs?"

"Yes, he's downstairs eating breakfast."

Kelly handed the baby back to her mom. "Can I go and eat breakfast with daddy before I get dressed.?"

"Yes, sweetheart, go right ahead."

Kelly ran downstairs to sit and eat breakfast with her dad before he headed off to work.

"Good morning daddy."

"Well, good morning sweet pea." Her dad said as he picked her up.

"How is my favorite girl?"

"Daddy, I'm tired. Do I have to go to school today? Why can't I stay home with mom and Chloe?"

"Because little girls your age have to attend school, if not, your mom and I could get in trouble. Is that what you want?"

"Oh no daddy, I don't want that."

Her dad laughed as he put her down. "Here take a seat while I fix you some breakfast and if you hurry up, I can take you to school on my way to work."

"Cool," Kelly said, grinning from ear to ear.

Later that afternoon, Katie put Chole down for her nap. She checked the baby monitor to make sure it was turned on and then she made her way downstairs to the family room where she had planned to watch her daily talk shows.

Katie had her lunch to the right of her and the baby monitor sat to the left. She grabbed the remote control and turned the volume up a little bit just to make sure she didn't miss anything that Blair Underwood had to say on the Wendy Williams show. She was all ready to listen when she heard static coming from the monitor. She picked the monitor up and turned the knob, just then she heard her neighbor next door arguing with her husband. By this time, Katie had forgotten all about her talk show.

Katie sat there for the next two hours listening to their conversation about her neighbor's husband cheating with the neighbor across the street.

"How dare you do this to me after all I have done for you. I have raised four of your children, help put your ass through medical school while holding down a job that I hated just so you could go to school and you cheat on me with that bitch across the street.

"Sally I don't have time for your bullshit today. You are always accusing me of sleeping with someone. Today it's the neighbor, next week it will be my assistant."

"Brian, I saw you this morning, leaving her house at 4 am."
Brian looked at his wife. "I'm busted, he thought to himself.'
   "Yeah, that's right. I saw you this morning."
   "I don't have time for this right now."
Brian said as he grabbed his keys and headed for the door.
   "You better make time for this or I'm filing for a divorce
and I will take everything you worked so hard for," Sally said
as she followed behind her husband.
Brian turned around and looked down at his wife.
   "Sally, you do whatever it is you want to do, but just know,
the judge will know about your drinking problem."
He said before walking out the front door.
   "You bastard."
Sally said as she threw the glass with her drink in it at the
door.
Just then, Chloe started crying.
   "Damn. This is getting good." She said out loud.
Katie ran upstairs to grab Chloe, she made her a bottle and
returned to her chair to feed her and to continue to listen to
her neighbors, but by this time, there was a different
conversation going on with two men. Katie turned the knob
several times, trying to find the conversation she was listening
to before, but she was unable to so she decided to listen to the
two men and try and to figure out who they were.
   "We have to play it cool so no one will suspect anything, if
not, you know what that means for us?" One of the men said.
   "I know, but you have to promise me, you won't say
anything to Frank. You know how big his mouth is."
   "Yeah, I know. He would love to see you behind bars."
   "Where are we going to hide this bag? It's so big and if we
take it outside and put it in our trunk, I know one of the
neighbors will surely see us and get suspicious."
   "I know. Let's just keep it down here until it starts to
smell."
Katie's eyes got big, "Oh my God! What are they talking
about?" She said as she continued to listen and feed Chloe.

A few minutes later, Katie puts Chloe in her swing as she continued to listen. The baby monitor jumped to another home. No!" she yelled as she tried to get back to that conversation, but instead it zeroed in on another home where nothing interesting was going on so Katie turned the knob again and it picked up the home of the cheating neighbor. She could hear the sound of someone crying, it sounded like the wife.

Sally sat at the kitchen table crying her heart out.

"That know good for nothing husband. I knew he was cheating with that slut across the street." Katie said.

Later that evening when Blake arrived home. Katie was there to greet him at the door. As Blake opened the front door, Katie pulled him inside quickly.

"Honey, I have got so news for you?" Katie said.

"Hey, sweetie, how was your day? My day was just great." Blake said sarcastically.

"Aw, I 'm sorry babe."

Katie reached up to kiss Blake on the lips.

"Here, let me take your things, oh by the way, how was your day?"

Blakes laughed at his wife. "It was good, but somehow, I think your day was even better."

"I'll tell you all about at dinner, no make that after dinner." Katie thought about her daughter and how she loved repeating things to her teacher and classmates.

"On my God! I forgot all about dinner," Katie said. "I was so busy listening to the monitor that I forgot to cook. Let me throw something together for dinner. Dinner will be ready in a little while.

Blake looked at his wife strangely. "You were listening to the monitor and forgot to cook dinner. How long were you listening and why were you listening to the monitor?"

"I will tell you all about it after dinner," Katie said smiling. She was so excited to tell Blake what she had heard.

At the dinner table, Blake told Katie about his day and how he was offered a position to head up a new company for Cummins.

"I hope this doesn't mean we have to move?"

"No, silly. I know moving is out of the question for you."

"Good, because I would hate to divorce you," Katie said, smiling.

After dinner, Katie and Blake moved to the family room while Kelly did her homework in Blake's office.

Katie couldn't wait to tell Blake about the things she heard today while listening to the baby monitor.

"Okay, sit back and listen. I was getting situated so I could watch the Wendy Williams show today because Blair Underwood was one of her guests when the monitor started messing up so I picked it up and turned the know when I heard a man and a woman arguing. I looked around and wondered where the voices were coming from when I realized it was coming from the monitor and guess who it was?"

Blake sighed. "Honey, I have no idea."

"It was Sally and Brian. He's been cheating on her with the lady across the street."

"No, that can't be. What about her husband?"

"Husband, she's not married."

"Who's the guy that drives the red corvette?"

"I have never seen a red corvette over there."

"Well, I have."

"Well, anyway. Sally told Brian that she was going to divorce him if he walked out and that she would take him for everything. He said and if you do, I will tell the judge about your drinking problem. Can you believe that?"

"And you heard all of that over the monitor?"

"Yes, and there's more. I heard two other people as well. Two men and I think they murdered someone."

 Blake shook his head. "Okay, that's it. You need to stop listening to other people's conversations. Blake said as he got up off the couch.

"I think I need some coffee. Would you like some?"

"Sure."

Katie followed her husband upstairs to the kitchen.

"You don't seem too worried about the thought of someone being murdered."

"Because I'm not so sure you heard what you think you heard. And where was Chloe when you were busy ease dropping on other people's conversations?"

"She was asleep at first and then I brought her down so I could feed here and then I placed her in her swing. And it's not like I was trying to ease drop. I was sitting there minding my own business."

"Do me a favor, please whatever you do, don't tell anyone what you think you heard."

"And why not?"

"Because this is how rumors get started. Besides, you have no clue who the men were and you have no proof that they murdered anyone."

CHAPTER TWO

That night, Blake awoke to find his wife missing from bed. He got up, checked on the girls and made his way downstairs where he found his wife sitting in the family room with the baby monitor.

Blake stood at the top of the stairs of the family room.

"What are you doing?"

Katie jumped at the sound of Blake's voice and dropped the monitor.

"Dang, you're always trying to scare someone."

Blake laughed. "You are so nosey. One day that nose of yours is going to get you in a whole lot of trouble. Come on back to bed."

"Alright, I'll be up in a minute."

Katie continued to sit with the monitor waiting to see if she could hear anything and just when she was about to turn it off, she heard a man's voice.

"You're such a pretty girl. I promise when I am done with you, you won't feel a thing."

Katie heard a female crying in the background.

"Please don't hurt me. I will do whatever you want, just don't hurt me."

The female's cry pulled at Katie's heart.

"Oh my God!"

Katie ran upstairs to her husband and told him what she had just heard.

Blake turned over, turned on the light and sat up in bed as he listened to his wife.

Blake ran his hand over his face.

"Blake we need to do something?"

"Honey, what can we do? We don't know who this person is or where he lives. What are we going to tell the police?"

"I don't know, but I know I just can't sit around and do nothing."

"If you want to do something, try recording the next conversation so you will at least have something the police can listen to and you won't sound like a complete idiot."
Blake reached over, turned the lights out and lay back down.

"Now go to sleep, please.

The next day, when Blake arrived home from work. He was greeted by four female friends of Katie's. He knew they were up to no good. Ever since Katie found the baby monitor in the attic, she
had been playing the closer. He just hoped she didn't cause any problems for the neighbors with her assumptions.

"Hello, ladies," Blake said.

"Hey Blake, how are you?" The 1st lady asked.

"Hello, Blake." The other ladies said.

"Hey, babe. How was your day?" Katie asked as she walked up to her husband, kissed him on the lips and took his briefcase.

"It was good."

"Are you hungry? Katie asked as she made her way into the kitchen to warm up his dinner.

"Yes, I am starving. What did you do today?" Blake asked as he took a seat at the kitchen table.

"Oh, nothing really."

"You mean to tell me you didn't listen in on our neighbors today?"
Blake already knew the answer to his question before he asked his wife. He wanted to know if she would be honest with him. Katie hesitated before answering. She didn't know if she should tell him that she and the ladies all heard the conversations as well or not.

"I listened a little today, but nothing interesting happened today, but I did have my tape recorder with me just in case I heard something."

"You didn't tell the ladies about this, did you?"

"No."

Um.. Blake said.

"So what did you hear today?"

"We heard, I mean I heard a conversation between Sally and Brian. Nothing important, though."

Blake looked at her suspiciously. When your friends leave, we need to talk.

"Okay."

The ladies listened to the conversation between Katie and Blake. They could tell he was not happy about them knowing about the baby monitor and that they listened to their neighbor's conversation.

Katie made her way back to the living room to join her friends.

"I think it's time for us to leave." The 1st lady said.

"Is he upset that we know about the monitor?" The 2nd lady mouthed.

"I think so, but it's cool," Katie whispered.

Katie hugged each lady and walked them to the door. She stood in the doorway, looking around at the houses on her street trying to guess whose house the young lady was being held captive at.

Two minutes later, Katie decided to shut the door. She felt so bad that she can't help that young girl. She only hoped and prayed that it was just a joke, but something inside her told her it was real.

Katie walked back to the kitchen and took a seat across from her husband.

"Babe, I thought we discussed that you would not tell anyone about the conversations you heard over the monitor." Katie looked at her husband.

"You know this could hurt people if your friends start spreading rumors. We all run in the same group. How would you feel if we were going through some things and it got out and our friends were talking about us behind out back?

"You're right, I didn't think about it like that."

"I think you need to put that baby monitor back where you found it and leave it alone."

Kelly ran down the stairs to the kitchen. "Mom, Chloe is awake."

"Did you wake her up?"

"No."

"Are up sure?" Katie asked as she hugged her daughter and started tickling her on her side.

"I'm sure, Mom." Kelly laughed.

"Oh, so my favorite girl is just going to ignore me. I am so hurt." Blake said.

Kelly ran to her dad. "Aw, so now you want to come to me after you have hurt my feelings. Oh, I don't think so. Go back over there to your mom."

"I'm sorry dad," Kelly said as she looked at her dad.

Blake laughed and grabbed her and pulled her to him and kissed her on the forehead.

"Let's go get Chloe and give your mom a break."

"Why thank you," Katie said while getting up from the table.

Blake and Kelly made their way upstairs, Katie remained standing in the kitchen thinking. She couldn't get the young lady's voice out of her mind.

Katie moved over to the patio and moved the blinds so she could see out. She stared out into the darkness. "How could someone be so cold hearted?" She thought to herself.

Blake walked up behind her with Chloe in his arms.

"Babe, are you okay?" Blake asked.

"Yes, I'm fine."

"You don't look fine."

"Blake I can't help but wonder who the young lady was. The one I heard on the monitor yesterday. I continued to wonder if she's still alive." She said as she turned to face her husband and baby girl with tears in her eyes.

"Honey, come here," Blake said as he opened his arm while holding Chloe in the other arm.

"You have got to stop worrying. It's probably nothing. Have you watched the news to see if a young girl has gone missing?"

"No, I haven't, but that's a good idea. I'll make sure I watch the news tonight or do you think I should call the police to see if there's a young girl missing?"

"No, I don't think calling the police will do any good. Do you know how many girls go missing every day? You have no description of the girl to give to the police."

"I know. I feel so helpless." She said as she laid her head against his chest.

"Oh my God! It almost slipped my mind. Did the realtor tell you about the family that lived here before us?' She asked as she raised her head off of his chest.

"No, why?"

"Helen told me today, that the family that lived here before us was murdered. She said she never mentioned it before because she thought we knew. I wonder if the monitor belonged to that family. I guess I need to do some research." Blake looked at his wife oddly. "Katie, please, don't do anything stupid and whatever you do, don't involve our neighbors. Now go downstairs and relax while Kelly and I take care of Chloe." Blake said as he kissed his wife on the lips and grabbed her ass.

"Yes, sir," Katie said as she saluted her husband. Katie sat downstairs in the family room trying to keep her mind occupied on the tv, but for some reason, she was unable to focus on the movie.

Katie turned her head sideways and looked at the baby monitor. She stared at it for a few seconds before reaching over to pick it up. Once she had it in her hands, she turned the monitor on and to her surprise, she heard the man who she swore had abducted a young lady, but what she heard was something very different from the last time.

"Daddy, can you come upstairs and read a book to me." The little girl asked.

"Sure, sweetheart. Just let me straighten up down here and I will be right up." The little girl ran upstairs to pick out her favorite book.

Katie could not believe what she just heard. "Maybe I was wrong." She said to herself.

The next morning, Katie got her daughter off to school and her husband off to work. She fed her little one and put her back to bed. She was busy doing her chores when she thought she heard a young lady calling out for help.

"Someone please help me." She screamed.

"Oh my God!" Katie ran to the front door with the monitor in her hand as if she was going to see the young lady inside the home.

Katie ran outside and stood on the sidewalk and looked around at the neighbors' homes, but running outside, caused her to lose the signal so she rushed back inside.

The young lady screamed and then she heard laughter. Katie was puzzled, was someone playing games with her or was the young lady really in trouble???

COMING IN 2017

WHEN IT RAINS

CHAPTER ONE

OCTOBER 29, 2015

When It Rains takes place in Seattle, Washington during the rainy season, which began in November and ended in the latter part of March. This year will be different for the townspeople of Seattle, Washington because they will be terrorized and hit with a series of murders that take place when it rains...

Darren Clark and his wife were preparing for the rainy season as they sat in their home going over plans for their trip to Atlanta.

Darren and his wife Felicia both work from home so they can pack up at any time and work from anywhere in the United States. Every year at this time, they left Seattle and returned when the rainy season was over. This year, his wife wanted to spend time with her family in Atlanta.

"Honey, I need to run into town and grab a few items. Do you need anything while I'm out?"

"No, I'm good."

Felicia grabbed her purse, keys and hopped in her jeep. She started the ignition, turned the radio on, and pulled out of the driveway almost hitting a man who stood in front of their driveway. Felicia slammed on her brakes, put the car in park, hopped out of the car and ran to the back of the jeep to find the man she almost hit on the ground.

"Are you okay? I am so sorry, but I didn't see you until it was almost too late."

"I'm okay, just a little shaken up."

Felicia helped the man up who had fallen to the ground when he heard the sound of her slamming on her brakes.

"You didn't hit me, it's just the sound of your brakes as you slammed on them frightened me and I wasn't paying any attention and tripped over these logs here." He said as he brushed the dirt off his pants and jacket.

"Are you sure you're okay? Can I get you something to drink?"

"Yeah, that would be nice.

"Come on in the house with me."

Felicia led the man into the house. She introduced the stranger to her husband.

"I almost ran him down in the driveway."

"Imagine that. I get on her all the time about speeding out of the driveway like a mad woman. I bet you will take my advice from now on."

"Oh, hush," Felicia said as she swatted her husband.

"Are you guys planning a trip?" The stranger asked.

Darren explained to the stranger about their adventure during the rainy season.

"When are you guys leaving?"

"We should be out of here by tomorrow night."

"When are you returning?"

"We should be back at the end of the rainy season. I can only take so much rain and drizzle. By the way, what's your name?"

The stranger hesitated for a moment, "my name is John."

"Well, it's nice to meet you, John." John shook Darren's hand.

Felicia walked over and handed John a glass of water.

"John, can I give you a lift somewhere? I was heading into town."

"That's where I was headed."

"Then I'll give you a lift into town."

John and Felicia were heading to town when a police officer pulled them over. John almost shit in his pants. It was obvious to Felicia by his actions that he was running from something.

"It's okay John he's a friend of my husband's." She said as she touched his hand.

John tried to relax, but had a hard time looking directly at the officer.

"What do we have here?" The officer asked Felicia

"What do you want Fred?"

"Where's Darren?"

"He's at home packing."

"That's right, you guys are getting ready to leave for a few months."

"Who do we have here?"

"His name is John. I'm giving him a ride into town."

"Can John speak for himself?"

"Yes, I can speak for myself. My name is John Robinson. I'm from Portland, Washington. Is there anything wrong with that?"

"So Felicia how do you know John?"

"I just met him when I almost ran him over in front of my driveway. Why do you ask?"

"There's been some talk in town about a stranger wandering around town."

"That would be me," John said. I've been looking for work in town."

"Have you had any luck?"

"No, I haven't."

"Where are you staying?" The police officer continued to question John. He had his suspicions about him.

"Here and there."

"Can we go now, Fred?"

"Sure. But John I will be keeping my eye on you."
John saluted the officer trying to be sarcastic.

"What was that about?" John asked.

"Oh, you have to overlook Fred. He's not too fond of outsiders."

The two finally made it to town. "John, where can I drop you off at?"

"I need to find work so I can stay in a hotel until I find a room to rent. So if you know of any place around here that may be hiring, then that will be a good place to start."
Felicia started to think. "We have a room you can rent and since we will be leaving town you can have the entire house to yourself, but I will have to ask Darren first, but if he says it's okay then you have a place to stay. Let me call him right now."
After hanging up with Darren, Felicia turned to face John.

"You're in luck. Darren said he would love to have you here, especially since we will be leaving. He doesn't like leaving our home unoccupied for a long period."

"Good that solves one of my problems."

"John I will reach out to a couple of friends that have their own business and see if we can get you a job. It shouldn't be a problem."

"Oh, my day is turning out to be fantastic," John said as he rubbed his hands together. "I don't know what I would have done if you hadn't almost run me over." He said as he laughed and looked over at Felicia

Felicia called two of her friends trying to get John a job but was unsuccessful. She was getting ready to call her friends Ralph and Sylvia when her phone rang.

"Hi Felicia, I almost forgot, we will need help in our store in a couple of weeks, so if your friend can wait until then, he has a job as a stocker."

"Thanks, Caroline I will let him know.

"It looks like fate is on your side today. You have a job at a Marsh supermarket in a couple of weeks.

"Thank you so much Felicia."

"Don't mention it."

John made himself comfortable as he wandered around the house familiarizing himself with his surroundings. He walked out back and followed a trail that led into the wooded area. He walked for about a mile when he walked upon a lake. John wondered if there were any fish in the lake. John loved the outdoors and was accustomed to spending nights in the outdoors as a kid, but not too much as an adult. His favorite pastime was fishing up until five years ago.

Five years ago, John was out fishing when a group of teenagers terrorized him. It was a quiet rainy evening and John camped out at a lake in Portland when a group of teenagers approached him. They beat John badly and took everything he had. He was in the hospital for two weeks and when he recovered, he vowed to get even with the hoodlums and he did. No one ever saw the group of teenagers again. So now, whenever it rains, it does something to John mentally.

John made his way back into the house, but just as he did it started to rain. John hated it when it rained. It caused him to act in a way he would not normally act.

CHAPTER TWO

John took a shower, changed into some clean clothes and made his way to the kitchen to prepare him some dinner.

John was in deep thought when he heard a car pulling up. At first, he thought it was Darren and Felicia, but when he heard a knock, he knew it was not them.

John made his way over to the door and opened it to find Fred standing there.

"What can I do for you, Fred?" John asked as he heard the sound of the lightning strike. John shook his head, trying to fight the feeling that went through his body when he heard the lightning.

"Can I come in out of the rain?"

"Sure, why not."

"So where did you say you come from?"

"Why are you harassing me? I just got into town and here you are already harassing me. Don't you have anything better to do?" John said as he closed the door behind him.

"I'm the law around here so don't question me."

"Well, I have rights and I have not done anything wrong, so don't come around him questioning me," John said as she stood face to face with Fred standing his ground. John was about 5 inches taller than Fred with a very muscular build.

"Do I need to haul your ass into town?" Fred was about to call in for back up when John moved closer to him.

"I'd like to see you try it," John said right before grabbing Fred around the neck twisting it causing it to break. John allowed Fred's body to fall to the ground.

"Damn, why did you make me do this to you?"

John left his body lying right there on the ground and went back to eating his dinner.

Later that night, John lit a fire in the fireplace to burn Fred's clothes. He then took Fred's body and carried it to the bathtub where he began to chop up his body into parts with an ax. Then he placed each part into the fire as Fred burned to ashes, but he left the head in the tub.

John searched the house for a plastic bag that would be big enough to hold Fred's head. Once he found the plastic bag, he put the head

inside the bag and buried in the backyard. He decided to hide the car, but before he had a chance to hide the car, the sound of rain and the thunder hit him again and the urge to kill was stronger than ever. No matter how hard he tried to fight this urge, he never ended up winning the fight.

John hopped in the sheriff's car, backed out of the driveway and headed in search of his next victim.

John searched neighborhood after neighborhood until he came across three girls walking down the street. He parked his car a few houses up and walked back to where he had seen the girls, but by the time he made it back, they had gone inside a three-story brick home.

John continued to linger around on the empty, deserted street hoping he would catch his prey for the night. He stood out in the pouring rain under the light pole hoping the girls would come back out. John pulled out a cigarette, lit it and paced back and forth until he realized he was wasting his time here. John continued to drive around and ended up at Al's Tavern. He walked in, surveyed the area and took off his jacket before heading to the bar.

"What can I get you to drink?" the bartender asked.

"I'll take a miller lite."

Again, John heard the thunder and he jumped.

"Here you go." The bartender said as she noticed John jump. "You're not from around here, are you?"

"No, why do you ask."

"I haven't seen you in here before." The bartender said, trying to flirt with John.

John noticed how the bartender kept eyeing him.

"What time do you get off?" John asked.

"Not until two."

"I'll be out back waiting for you," John said as he drank down the rest of his beer. He laid a twenty on the bar as a tip.

"I'll be the one in the police car," John said as he leaned over the bar and whispered in the bartender's ear.

The bartender winked and went about her business.

Hours later, John awoke when the bartender approached the car.

"So you're a cop?" The bartender said as she touched him.

"Yeah, you got a problem with it?"

"I don't like cops."

"Neither do I," John said as he started the car.

"Get in."

"So what's your name?" John asked.

"Regina, but you can call me Gina."

"So what's your name Mr. Police Officer?"

"I'm John."

"Where are we going?"

"We're going to my place. I hope you don't mind?"

"No, that's cool."

The two rode in silence until John pulled into the driveway.

"Hey, this is Darren and Felicia's house," Gina said.

"I know I'm staying here until they return in the spring."

"Um..." Something doesn't seem right to Gina. " I've changed my mind. Can you take me back to the bar?"

John laughed.

"Are you serious? John asked as he cut the engine. You should be more careful about getting into cars with people you don't know. Now get your ass out of the car." John said calmly.

Inside the house, John fought with himself. He tried his best to fight off the urge to kill Gina.

"So what do you want to do?" John said, trying to calm Gina's nerves.

"Just so you know, I would never hurt you or do anything to you that you don't want me to do," John said as he stood up. Gina walked up to John and put her hand on his chest.

"Whatever you want to do big boy is fine with me."

John picked Gina up and carried her to his bedroom. He laid her down on the bed and undressed as she watched. When he was finished, he undressed her and crawled between her legs. He ran his penis up and down her pussy before entering her.

"Aw, daddy you're a big boy."

"Do you like it?"

"Yes daddy, I love it."

John began to stroke her harder and deeper. He moved his hands to her throat where he began to choke her. He held her so tight that tears began to flow from her eyes. Gina tried her best to get John's hands from around her neck. She screamed and moved her legs trying to get him off her, she even tried moving his hands, but she was unsuccessful.

John continued to pump her with his hands still wrapped around her neck. When he came, he removed his hands from around her neck and laid his body on top of her, unfortunately for Gina, her life had ended.

John laid there for a minute before taking Gina's dead body into the bathtub where he chopped her body into pieces and threw them into the burning fire. He did the same thing to her head as he had done to Fred. Now he had two heads buried in the backyard.

John knew he had to get rid of the police car as soon as possible. So in the meantime, he pulled the car around back until the morning.

ABOUT THE AUTHOR

Denise Hill was born and raised in Indianapolis, IN where she resides with her son Daniel and her daughter Devin. Denise attended Thomas Carr Howe High School and received her degree in Business from the University of Phoenix. Denise started writing at the age of 14 where she won a trip to Tronto, Canada and Washington, DC. She went on to publish three novels titled Love of a Lifetime, Double Crossed and Scandalous. Denise has ventured into films as well as a screenwriter, acting, producing movies and directing. She's a radio talk show host and one of the founders and is the President of MEA. Denise has produced a short film titled Abducted, Web Series called Love of a Lifetime and coming soon she will do her first audio Webseries for her novel Scandalous. She is currently working on a featured film titled The House Guest. She has other movie projects that she will be working on as well as an online magazine titled MEA Life and soon she will showcase her own swimwear line for regular and plus size women. Denise is the owner of DH Publishing & Production Company, where she helps people bring their dream of being a writer a reality.

Upcoming novels:

The Monitor
When It Rains
Torn
The Other Man
Because He Loves Me
Because of You
The Ultimate Betrayl
A Cold Winter Night

ENVY

Denise Hill

www.ingramcontent.com/pod-product-compliance
Lightning Source LLC
Chambersburg PA
CBHW070337260626
47160CB00003B/1071